# Running in her shadow

**Robert Rigby**

## About the author

Robert Rigby is best known for writing the bestselling *Boy Soldier* series with Andy McNab. He began his career as a journalist, then turned to writing for radio, television and the theatre and has also directed and performed in children's theatre throughout the country. He wrote the novelizations of the movies, *Goal!* and *Goal II*, and a third novel in the series, *Goal: Glory Days*. His scripts for television include the long-running BBC children's drama, *Byker Grove*.

**ALSO IN THIS SERIES**

*Parallel lines*

# Running in her shadow

**An official
London 2012 novel**

**Robert Rigby**

CARLTON
BOOKS

First published by Carlton Books Limited 2011
Copyright © 2011 Carlton Books Limited

London 2012 emblems: ™ & ® The London Organising Committee of the Olympic Games
and Paralympic Games Ltd (LOCOG) 2007.
London 2012 Pictograms © LOCOG 2009. All rights reserved.

Carlton Books Limited, 20 Mortimer Street, London, W1T 3JW.

A CIP catalogue record for this book is available from the British Library.

10 9 8 7 6 5 4 3 2 1

ISBN: 978-1-84732-763-5

Printed in the UK by CPI Mackays, Chatham, ME5 8TD

FSC
MIX
Paper
FSC® C020471

# One

Megan felt fantastic. Amazing. Brilliant.

Sometimes when Megan ran at top speed, hurtling towards the finish line in a 100-metres race or leaning into the bend in the longer sprint, she felt almost as if she could fly. It was like she was accelerating down a runway so fast, with her feet barely touching the ground, that at any second she would lift off and go soaring away into the clouds.

It was an incredible feeling – the best – and that was how Megan had been feeling all day. In fact, it was how she'd been feeling all weekend.

It was partly because she was at the top of her form – sprinting as well, if not better, than ever before. But it was also because she was part of something new and exciting – a special training weekend for talented young athletes.

Megan Morgan was nearly fourteen and her dream was to compete one day in the Olympic Games. And she believed that this weekend was an important step towards making that dream come true.

Ever since receiving her invitation, Megan had been impatiently counting down the days until the last Friday before her weekend away. When it finally arrived, and when an endless day at school was finally over, Megan's mum, Anne, drove her from their home near Wrexham in North Wales to Manchester, where the event was taking place.

Megan was almost bursting with excitement during the journey. And so was Anne.

Anne had once been an athlete, too: a hurdler, good enough to run for Wales in the Commonwealth Games. Now she coached her daughter, and she believed that Megan was going to become a top international athlete.

'You'll listen carefully to everything the coaches tell you, won't you?' Anne said as they reached Manchester. 'They'll be some of the very best, so do exactly as they say.'

'Yes, Mum.'

'And make sure you do a proper warm-up, and a warm-down at the end of each training session.'

'Yes, Mum.'

'We don't want any pulled muscles or hamstring injuries.'

'No, Mum,' Megan answered, with a smile, realising that her mum was excited and a little nervous, too.

Megan had been running for as long as she could

remember. She had often looked at her mum's medals and listened to the stories about her best races. But it was watching the 2008 Olympic Games on television and seeing the incredible, world-record shattering runs of the Jamaican sprinter, Usain Bolt, that had really inspired her to take athletics seriously.

The Lightning Bolt, as he was called, not only ran faster than anyone else on the planet, he hurtled down the track with a huge smile on his face. Megan could almost feel his joy as he gave television interviews after the races. She wanted to feel the same joy when she ran. Sometimes, when she was at her very best, she thought that she did. And now her special talent was beginning to be noticed.

Anne parked the car and they went into the reception area where other youngsters were arriving and being signed in.

Megan had been to sleepovers at friends' houses and stayed with grandparents, but this was different. It felt more grown-up, somehow. Anne was much more anxious about it than her daughter. 'You'll be all right, won't you?' she said, hugging Megan tightly.

'I'll be fine, Mum, really.'

'And you're not worried about being on your own?'

'I'm not on my own; there are loads of other people here. You're squeezing me really tightly, Mum. I can hardly breathe.'

'Sorry,' Anne said, releasing her daughter and stepping back. She smiled. 'I'd better go, then.'

Megan nodded. 'Yep, see you on Sunday.'

Anne turned away and went to leave. But just before she reached the door she turned back. 'You will call tomorrow, won't you? Your phone is fully charged?'

'Yes and yes,' Megan said, grinning.

'Right,' Anne said, 'I'm off. You have a wonderful weekend.'

And Megan did have a wonderful weekend; she loved every minute, every second.

The young athletes, girls and boys, were each allocated a coach to work with on this and on future weekends. Megan's coach was a former international sprinter called Carole, who Megan guessed was about the same age as her mum. Carole was very relaxed and smiley and kind. And when she spoke to all the new sprinters about the training weekend, she was really encouraging, too. Megan liked her instantly.

Then there were the other athletes, not just sprinters but middle- and long-distance runners as well as jumpers and throwers. They were all aged between thirteen and fifteen. Some were first-timers like Megan, while others had been to previous training weekends.

On the first evening the young athletes formed little groups, to chat and share their stories. The sprinters were in one group, the middle- and long-distance runners made up another, while the field eventers – jumpers and throwers – also gathered together. Everyone had something to say, and Megan gradually found herself joining in the conversations.

One of the other sprinters was a fifteen-year-old girl called Katy, who came from Liverpool. Katy had lots to say but seemed especially good at listening, too. And when she realised that Megan was feeling a little shy and awkward, she came and sat beside her and gave her a reassuring smile. Everyone was talking about favourite athletes and Megan hadn't yet felt brave enough to name hers.

'Who's yours, Megan?' Katy said with a smile.

'It's … it's Usain Bolt. I think he's incredible.'

'Oh, yes!' Katy said, raising one hand to give Megan a high five. 'Legend! He's my favourite, too.'

From then on, the girls were firm friends.

Training the following day was amazing. All the athletes warmed up together before dividing into groups for specialist work. The coaching was brilliant: tough and challenging but never too tough nor too challenging. Megan kept reminding herself that when she got home she must tell her mum about everything she'd learned.

That evening there were talks by star athletes, some very familiar and famous names. Then there was a film showing great Olympic champions, like Sebastian Coe and Kelly Holmes winning their gold medals.

It was all so exciting and thrilling. The weekend passed in a flash, like a one-hundred-metre sprint, and much too quickly for Megan's liking. On the Sunday morning she found herself wishing she could start it all over again.

That afternoon, after all the serious training and hard work, the coaches organised some fun relay races, with athletes teaming up to race against each other.

Megan and Katy made sure they were in the same team, and two more girls, who were both fourteen, completed their quartet. Even though the coaches reminded all the runners that the relays were just for fun, everyone wanted to win and impress them as well as enjoy themselves.

Megan's race was the last of the day. She was running the third leg and would be passing the baton to Katy for the final leg. There had been no time to practise, so everyone was just running flat out and hoping for the best when it came to passing the baton from one runner to the next.

The race started and Megan watched excitedly, hopping nervously from foot to foot, as the lead runners set off. It was a fairly even first hundred metres, and at the first change over Megan's team was fifth of the eight teams. Some of the change overs were good and some not so good; the team in fourth place dropped their baton and Megan's team moved up a place.

Megan crouched, poised and ready, one arm reaching back, as the second girl in her team hurtled towards her, nearer and nearer. Megan began to run, not looking behind, but with her arm reaching back, palm upwards, ready to receive the baton. As she felt it slap into her hand, her fingers closed around the cylinder and gripped it tightly. She had the baton safely. Now all she had to do was sprint as fast as she possibly could.

She was in fourth place as she set off but Megan ran a blistering leg, streaking past two rivals, one outside her and one on the inside lane. As she approached the waiting Katy, there was only one runner ahead of their team.

Megan saw Katy start to run and pick up speed, arm stretched back, as she closed in. Megan reached out with the baton, Katy's fingers closed around it and it passed perfectly from one girl to the other.

'Go, Katy, go!' yelled Megan as her new friend streaked down the final straight towards the finish line.

Katy, all power and movement, closed on the leading girl and ten metres from the finish line edged to the front. She crossed the line half a metre ahead.

'We've won, we've won!' Megan screamed, leaping into the air and clapping her hands, before running off to join her team mates. 'We've won!'

# Two

'So, come on then. Tell us all about it.'

'Mum,' Megan said, 'I've already told you twice.'

It was breakfast time on Monday morning. Megan's dad, John, was eating a slice of toast. 'She has told us, love,' he said to Anne, wiping crumbs from his lips. 'Let's change the subject, eh?'

'No,' Anne said. 'I need to know all the details. It's important.'

'But I've told you all the details,' Megan said. 'There's nothing more to tell.'

John got up and went to the kitchen worktop. 'More toast, anyone?' he asked, slipping two slices of bread into the toaster.

Anne put down the mug she was holding. 'What about the training?' she said to Megan. 'Is there anything you haven't told me about the training routines?'

'Anne!' John said. 'Will you please give the girl a break and calm down? Relax.'

'Relax!' said Anne. 'We don't have time to relax,

not for a second. This is just the start for Megan. From now on she has to work harder than ever, if she really wants to get to the top.'

'If *she* wants to?' John said.

Anne stared at her husband. 'What do you mean by that?'

'Nothing.'

'Yes, you do. Come on; say what you're thinking.'

They looked at each other, neither speaking, with Megan not knowing what to say. This was an argument she had heard before.

Megan's dad was a big sports fan, too. He liked athletics and rugby, but football was his favourite. Like many people from their part of Wales, he supported Liverpool Football Club. But John believed that sport was more about having fun than about winning, and he thought that sometimes Anne pushed their daughter too hard. Anne disagreed.

The awkward silence in the kitchen was suddenly broken as the bread in the toaster popped up.

John reached for his jacket, which was draped over the back of the chair he'd been sitting on. 'Don't think I'll bother with that toast now.' He looked at his watch. 'I'm late, anyway.'

He leaned down and kissed Megan on the cheek. Then he kissed Anne, too. 'See you both later.'

'Bye, Dad,' Megan said.

'Bye,' Anne said, picking up her coffee mug.

John went out and a few moments later they heard the car start and move off from the driveway. Megan and her mum sat in silence, both finishing their breakfast.

Anne sipped her coffee. She looked at Megan over the top of her mug and shrugged her shoulders slightly, as if to say, 'It wasn't my fault.'

Megan sighed.

Later, at school, Megan stood in the playground at break time with her two best friends, Ellie and Beth. Neither girl was big on sport, but they both knew how important it was to Megan, so they listened with interest and asked one or two questions as she told them about her exciting weekend.

As soon as she was sure Megan had finished her story, Ellie was ready with news of her own. 'We had a great time on Saturday afternoon,' she said.

'What did you do?' Megan asked.

'Me and Beth went down to the town centre,' Ellie said. 'On the bus.'

'Oh, right. Then what?'

'Well, we…' Ellie turned to Beth with a puzzled look on her face. 'What did we do then?'

'Looked in the shops,' said Beth.

'Oh, yeah. We looked in the shops.'

'Then we went and had a burger.'

'Yeah, we went and had a burger,' Ellie said. 'And a Coke.'

'I left half my burger because Gavin Richards and his lot came in,' Beth said. 'Making as much noise as they could.'

'They're always showing off,' Ellie said. 'So we left and went back to the shops.'

Megan nodded. It didn't sound like the most thrilling afternoon ever, but she wasn't going to say that to her two friends. 'Did you buy anything?'

This was the bit that Ellie was clearly bursting to tell, but she saw the warning look from Beth and they both shook their heads.

'No,' Beth said. 'Not a thing.'

'No, nothing,' Ellie confirmed. 'Nothing at all.'

'Oh,' said Megan. She smiled. It was just four days to her birthday, when Ellie and Beth were coming to Megan's house for a sleepover. And from the secretive looks her friends were exchanging, Megan suspected that they might have bought her a present during their afternoon out.

'So you didn't buy anything at all, then?' she asked mischievously.

'Don't keep asking,' Beth said quickly.

'It's a secret,' Ellie said.

'Shhhh,' Beth said to Ellie.

'What's a secret?' Megan asked.

'Nothing!' both girls said together.

Megan laughed. 'All right, I won't say another word. But I'm really looking forward to the sleepover.'

'So are we,' said Beth, who seemed pleased to be moving away from the subject of shopping.

'D'you know what presents you're getting?' Ellie asked.

Beth glared at her, but Ellie didn't seem to notice.

'I've got no idea,' Megan said.

Ellie looked amazed. 'Really? I always give my mum and dad a list. Then I know I'll get what I want.'

The bell for the end of break sounded and the three girls headed back to the main school building.

'Double maths,' Beth said gloomily as they joined the other pupils squeezing through the open doorway and into the corridor. 'It's not fair. It shouldn't be allowed on a Monday morning.'

'Boring,' Ellie said. She looked at Megan. 'I was thinking, Meg,' she said, 'about Friday…'

'What about it?'

'You're not going to talk about presents again, are you?' Beth said, giving Ellie another warning look.

'No, it's about Megan's mum.'

'My mum? What about her?' said Megan.

'She...' Ellie hesitated, as if uncertain whether she should go on.

'What about my mum, Ellie?' Megan asked.

'Well, she ... she won't talk about athletics all night, will she?'

# Three

It was a bit like landing in water, except that it was sand, and instead of the sea or a swimming pool, Megan's feet splashed down into the long-jump pit. As both feet dug into the smooth surface, millions of grains of sand flew off in every direction, like tiny drops of water.

'Good jump, Megan,' her mum said. 'Excellent.'

Megan got to her feet, brushing sand from her legs and shorts. She looked back to the take-off board and then at the spot where she had landed. 'Don't you want to measure it? See how far I jumped?'

'I'm not interested in distance at the moment,' her mum said with a shake of her head.

'But it was a good jump. You said so.' Megan looked back at the pit. 'I think it was probably my longest yet.'

Anne picked up a rake lying close to the pit and began to smooth the sand, wiping away all traces of Megan's jump. 'All I'm worried about at the moment is your technique: speed on the runway, take-off, kick and landing. It was all pretty good that time. Get it right every time and the distance will come when it really matters.'

Megan nodded. 'So shall I do another one?'

'No, that's enough for this evening. Always finish on a high, eh? We'll do a gentle warm-down.'

Megan slipped on her tracksuit and they both began to jog slowly around the athletics club track. The other athletes who had been out training had gradually disappeared as the evening wore on and they had it to themselves now.

'I really do believe that one day you'll make a great heptathlete,' Anne said, as they jogged past the stadium's small grandstand.

Megan wasn't so sure. 'I dunno about that, Mum,' she said. 'Seven different events over two days sounds impossible.'

'Of course it's not impossible,' said Anne. 'You're already a top-class sprinter for your age, your hurdling is excellent and your long jump is improving all the time. You're growing taller so there's every chance you'll be a decent high-jumper, and when you get a little older, and stronger, we'll try the throwing events, to see how you get on.'

'I can't see me ever throwing the javelin or putting the shot,' said Megan. 'I'm too weedy for that.'

'You're not weedy,' Anne said, laughing. 'And you'll get stronger as you grow. Anyway, all heptathletes have some events that are better than others. Even the greats.'

'Like Denise Lewis.'

'Exactly.'

Just as Usain Bolt was Megan's favourite athlete, Denise Lewis was her mum's. The British athlete won the Heptathlon gold medal over two gruelling days at the 2000 Olympic Games in Sydney.

'Even Denise had her weaker events,' Anne went on, 'but she was determined to win that gold medal, and she did. You show the same determination and maybe one day you'll be even better than Denise Lewis.'

Megan laughed. 'Some hope!'

'Or Jessica Ennis,' her mum said, joining in with the laughter.

Megan knew all about Jessica Ennis, the young British athlete who'd become world Heptathlon champion in 2009 and European champion the following year – and was favourite for the gold medal at the fast approaching London 2012 Olympic Games.

'I can't wait to see her at London 2012,' Megan said.

'Neither can I,' Anne added. 'I am so looking forward to these Games; they'll be fantastic. And then maybe you'll be at the Games after that, competing for Great Britain.'

They were just about to complete a full lap of the track, and that was plenty for Megan. She was a lot less keen on running long distances than she was on shorter sprints. 'Doesn't the Hepthalon finish with an eight-hundred-metres race – two whole laps?' she asked.

Her mum nodded. 'That's the tough one. Come on, let's do one more lap now.'

Megan groaned.

On the way home in the car, Anne was still talking about great athletes like Denise Lewis and her other favourite, Colin Jackson.

'The greatest Welsh hurdler ever,' she said. 'One of the world's best ever.'

'But he never won an Olympic gold medal, did he?' Megan asked. She knew the answer, but she also knew that her mum enjoyed talking about the great Colin Jackson.

Anne shook her head sadly. 'Everything else: two world championships, the world record, European titles. But he never got that Olympic gold. Shows how hard it is at the very top of world athletics. But he was wonderful to watch, especially for another hurdler like me. Perfect technique, terrific speed and fantastic rhythm. Beautiful.'

There was a question Megan had wanted to ask her mum for some time and now seemed the right moment. 'Mum, why did you give up athletics? You were still young. You could have gone on for much longer.'

Anne sighed. 'It was after the Commonwealth Games. I was so proud to represent Wales.'

'I would be, too.'

'I got through the first round, just, but then I went out in the second. Some of the other athletes were so much better than me; they were a different class.'

'But that didn't mean you had to stop completely.'

'I wanted to be a winner, Megan. And I knew I'd never be quite good enough to have a chance of winning at the very highest level. I'd never be top class. So I stopped. I didn't want to be an also-ran.'

They were silent for a few moments as Megan thought over what her mum had said.

Then Anne spoke. 'Now you, you're different. I know that already. You're going all the way to the very top. And when you do, I shall be so, so proud.'

Megan suddenly felt anxious. She loved running. And racing. And she wasn't happy when she lost a race. But sometimes her future in athletics seemed even more important to her mum than it was to Megan herself.

'Shall we talk about Friday?' she said. 'What time shall I tell Ellie and Beth to come round?'

'Oh, there's plenty of time to think about Friday,' Anne replied. 'Let me tell you about the time Colin smashed the world record. It was the most fantastic run.'

# Four

Megan's dad reckoned that the wobbly, warbling high notes he was singing were the harmony to 'Happy Birthday To You'.

Everyone else stuck to the melody. Megan poked her fingers in her ears as John went for a particularly high note and Anne said he sounded more like a frightened cat than a singer. Ellie and Beth were laughing by the time they reached the final line, and as the last note echoed away, Megan took a deep breath and began to blow out the fourteen candles on her cake.

'Make a wish,' Ellie said.

One stubborn candle was still flickering so Megan blew harder until finally it spluttered out. 'I did,' she said.

'What did you wish for?' asked Ellie.

'She can't tell you, can she?' Beth said. 'Otherwise it won't come true.'

'Do you believe in all that stuff?' said Ellie.

Megan's mum put some plates on the table. 'Of

course she does. We all do, don't we?' She pulled the candles from the cake and handed Megan a knife. 'Cut your cake, Meg. I made a wish for you, too.'

'Bet I can guess what that was about,' John said.

Anne glanced at her husband, but ignored his comment.

Megan was enjoying her birthday evening. Just as she had suspected, and just as Ellie had been dying to tell her all week, the two girls had been shopping for a birthday present the previous Saturday. They'd combined their money and bought Megan a top from a clothes store that they all loved. Megan was delighted. She ran up to her bedroom to try it on and came down wearing it.

'Gorgeous!' said Ellie.

Then the girls admired Megan's other presents and read her cards, including one from her new friend, Katy.

Anne had made a birthday party tea. There were sandwiches and little sausages and cubes of cheese and pineapple on sticks. Anne said it was the sort of birthday tea she'd loved when she was their age and the girls loved it, too.

Then Anne decided it was time for the birthday cake. They all watched Megan take the knife and go to plunge it into cake.

Suddenly the doorbell chimed.

'At last,' John said. 'This was meant to arrive half an hour ago.' He smiled as he saw the puzzled look on all four faces. 'Just wait here and don't do anything to that poor, helpless cake until I get back.'

He left the room and Megan looked at her friends, shrugging her shoulders as she put down the knife. 'I've no idea what's going on. You can never tell with my dad.'

A few moments later they all knew exactly what was going on as John returned to the room carrying a huge, flat box.

'Pizza!' said the three girls in unison.

'One extra-large Margherita,' John said, placing the box onto the table. 'It's so late, I thought you might have to eat it after your birthday cake.'

Anne didn't look pleased. 'Oh, John!' she said.

'What? It's her favourite. I wanted to give them a surprise.'

'But what about the cake and the food they've already eaten and all the fizzy stuff they've been drinking? Now pizza! Megan shouldn't be eating all this. She's got an important race next weekend.'

'Mum!' Megan said. 'It's my birthday. Don't spoil it, please. The race is a week away and a few slices of pizza won't hurt me.'

Ellie reached over and opened the box. The rich smell of melted cheese filled the room. 'Don't worry, Mrs.

Morgan,' she said with a grin. 'If you really don't think she should have any, I can probably manage Megan's share too.' She grinned. 'And you don't want to get melted cheese on your new top, do you, birthday girl?'

Megan ate her pizza without getting a single speck of cheese on her new top. The girls polished off the whole thing, followed by large slices of birthday cake. Then Megan told her parents that they were going to watch a DVD.

The three girls trooped into the living room, sank onto the sofas and were soon engrossed in the rom-com movie they had specially chosen. Ellie, who had managed the biggest share of pizza, was asleep in minutes.

The film was almost finished when the living room door opened a little and Anne looked in. 'Everyone all right?' she asked.

'Fine,' Megan whispered, trying not to wake the sleeping Ellie. She put a finger to her lips.

'Maybe you should all turn in soon, eh?' Anne said quietly. 'You know you need plenty of sleep, Megan. Training tomorrow.'

'In a while,' Megan replied. 'We'll see the end of this and then go up.'

Anne nodded and closed the door. Megan glanced over at Beth, who was giving her a meaningful look. She didn't need to put her thoughts into words.

'I know,' Megan whispered, feeling a little embarrassed. 'Mum just wants me to do well, that's all.'

'Yeah,' Beth replied, looking at her watch. 'But it's not late and you are fourteen now.' She grinned. 'Just.'

Megan smiled. 'At least she didn't make us watch the videos of me winning races.'

'Oh no!' said Beth throwing up her hands in mock horror.

Both girls started to giggle and then Ellie turned in her sleep and gave a loud snore.

Megan and Beth's giggles erupted into loud laughter, which immediately woke up Ellie. She sat up, rubbed her eyes and stared sleepily at her two friends. 'What?' she said, looking completely bewildered.

The two girls just laughed even louder.

# Five

Megan loved the buzz of an athletics meeting. There was always something happening. Wherever you looked, wherever you went, there was movement and variety. Athletics, for Megan, was the most exciting sport in the world.

She watched as the leaders in a 1500-metres race went panting by, approaching the start of the last lap, jostling for position, bunching up, all waiting to make their final burst for the finish line.

On the far side of the stadium, a long-jumper pounded down the runway towards the take-off board. In the shot-put circle, an athlete grunted loudly as he launched the heavy ball into the air and then shouted with pleasure as it thudded onto the ground.

There was so much for the spectators and the athletes to see.

As she warmed up for her own race, Megan was thinking that at the very earliest Olympic Games the scene would have been very similar, with athletes running, jumping or throwing while spectators watched and cheered. It was amazing to think that over thousands of years, the sport had hardly changed at all.

It was still early in the athletics season, but getting late in the school year, and today's was an important race. It was the county schools' championships and Megan was running in the final of the girls' 100 metres for under-15s. Even though she'd come through her qualifying heat comfortably, Megan was young for her school year, which meant that some of the girls competing would be nearly a year older than her. She wasn't overawed. She was nervous, but she always was before a big race. Not too nervous, just 'nicely nervous', as her mum called it.

There were competitors from almost every school in the county at the meet, and a club stadium with a proper track and facilities was being used for the occasion. It was crammed full of school students and parents who'd come to support their favourites. There was a terrific atmosphere and it was a great day for athletics – warm but not too hot, with virtually no wind to slow or help performances.

As Megan finished her warm-up, she heard a roar from the spectators on the far side of the stadium as a young high-jumper cleared the bar with ease.

Megan jogged over to her mum and dad who were near the finish line. As it was a schools' meet, Anne wasn't allowed to be in the centre of the arena; the coaching was strictly in the hands of the schools' own sports teachers.

Anne was clutching her video camera, ready to add to her collection of Megan movies. 'All right, Meg?' she asked, looking more nervous than Megan felt.

'Fine,' Megan said. When she was about to race, Megan usually said very little.

'You can win this, no problem.'

Megan just smiled.

'No pressure then, Meg?' said John with a wink. 'You just do your best and enjoy the race. Doesn't matter where you finish, just enjoy it.'

Megan saw her mum glare at her dad. The last thing she needed at that moment was another tense situation between them. 'I'd better get down to the start,' she said. 'They'll be calling us in a minute.'

A few minutes later Megan stood behind the start line with seven other girls. She was in lane three, which was good; she preferred being in a centre rather than outside lane.

'On your marks!'

The starter's voice came loudly through the speaker and a hush fell over the stadium. The girls moved forward and one by one got down into their starting positions. Some were quick to settle; others twitched and fidgeted before finally being still. Quicker than the rest, Megan made sure that her feet were firmly placed and that her hands were just behind the start line. She was ready.

'Set.'

All eight girls rose, poised to spring into action. The crowd was totally silent.

Crack!

The starter's pistol sounded and the competitors leapt away as the crowd erupted into shouts and cheers.

Megan moved like lightning and was swiftly up and into her stride. She was totally focused on her running; all she could hear was the distant roar of cheering as she concentrated on staying relaxed and sprinting as fast as she knew she could.

For a few strides Megan was aware of someone close to her on her left, but as she gathered speed the other girls seemed to drop away. When she crossed the finish line she was a good two metres clear of the girl in second place. A huge smile spread over her face as she slowed and went straight to where her mum and dad were jumping up and down with excitement.

'You did it!' Anne shouted. 'I knew you'd do it.'

'Brilliant, Meg!' John yelled. 'I'm so proud of you.'

Megan hugged them both and then turned back to shake hands with the other competitors. Before she had taken a couple of steps one of the officials came running over from the finish line.

'Congratulations, Megan,' he said. 'Fantastic run. And you've broken the record.'

Megan looked back to her parents. 'Did you hear that, Mum? I've broken the under-fifteen record.'

'And not just broken it,' said the beaming official. 'You've smashed it.'

Anne turned to her husband wearing a look of triumph. 'Pressure? What pressure? Our daughter thrives on pressure!'

# Six

Megan's record-breaking run was big news.

There was a story in the local newspaper with a photograph of Megan proudly showing off her winner's medal. In assembly at school, the headmaster gave her a special mention and everyone applauded and cheered. And she also received a phone call from Carole, her coach at the training weekend.

Carole, like everyone, was delighted with Megan's success. 'You must be very proud,' she said. 'It's great to break a record.'

'It was so embarrassing at school,' Megan told the coach. 'People I don't even know kept coming up to congratulate me. A boy in year eleven even asked for my autograph. He was only joking, but my friends said I went really red.'

Carole laughed. 'And I bet your mum and dad are thrilled?'

Megan hesitated before answering. 'Yes, they are.'

There was another pause before Carole spoke. 'Megan?' she asked. 'Is everything okay with your parents?'

'It's just that...' Megan hesitated again. She wasn't sure what to say. She had been worrying about the completely different ways her parents felt about her athletics for some time. But she'd tried to push her worries to the back of her mind, hoping they would go away.

'Yes?' Carole said gently.

'Mum and Dad,' Megan said at last, 'they ... they see it differently, my athletics. Mum is ... sort of ... desperate for me to win. And Dad...' She paused again, but only briefly this time. 'Dad just wants me to enjoy athletics and have fun. Not take it quite so seriously, I guess.'

'I'm absolutely sure they both want what's best for you,' Carole said.

'I know,' Megan agreed.

'Let's have a chat about it next time I see you?' Carole said. 'I know how difficult it can be keeping everyone happy all the time, especially parents.'

Megan smiled. Carole's gentle, quiet manner was just what she needed.

Carole turned the conversation back to athletics and to next weekend's training event. And by the time they ended their conversation, Megan felt bright and cheerful again.

But as she put down the telephone, it was probably a good thing that Megan couldn't see the concerned look on Carole's face.

The record-breaking run seemed to have made Anne even more determined to get the very best from her daughter and she increased Megan's training over the next couple of weeks.

Most of the time Megan enjoyed it, knowing that to get to the top she had to put in the effort. But sometimes, even Megan thought her mum was pushing just a bit too hard and putting her athletics before everything else.

Her dad was completely different, almost the total opposite, in fact. John didn't seem to care at all about winning. Even when he got the chance to see Liverpool play, he told Megan that he didn't care too much if they won or lost, as long as he saw a good game of football. He was proud of Megan when she won, but she knew that he would have been just as proud if she'd finished last. And sometimes, Megan found that frustrating, too. She loved running, simply for the great feeling it gave her, but she also wanted to win every race.

It was all very confusing. And when she thought about it, Megan realised that she didn't know how she should feel about it. And she couldn't ask either of her parents, because they thought so differently. Her mum was serious and determined and very sensible, while her dad often made a joke of even serious things. But he could be great fun, too. He liked to laugh, and so did Megan.

Megan thought that she must be a bit like both her parents, but she found herself thinking more and more that she wished her mum could sometimes be a little less serious and that her dad could sometimes be a little more serious. But that didn't look as though it would ever happen. Megan finally decided she just had to accept that they were different and try not to let it bother her.

So she concentrated all her thoughts and all her efforts on her athletics. And it seemed to pay off because the following weekend she won the junior long-jump event at an inter-club match.

'We're doing really well this season – even better than I'd hoped,' Anne said when they were at home that evening.

John was watching the television. He looked up. 'So does that mean Megan gets the chance to take it easy for a bit?'

'What do you mean?' asked Anne.

'She's been training so hard, I just thought that

maybe you could give her a bit of a break. It's about time she had some fun with her friends.'

Megan was staying out of the conversation. She didn't want it to turn into an argument. It was true though. Apart from school, Megan had seen very little of Ellie and Beth since her birthday.

Anne shook her head. 'It isn't just about having fun.'

But John wasn't giving up. 'And we haven't had a night out in ages. A little break would probably do you both good.'

'We can't afford to let up on training,' Anne said.

'But surely a few days off won't make any difference.'

'It could make all the difference. Megan realises how important it is to keep to her training routine, even if you don't.'

Both parents looked at Megan, as if they both wanted her to support their point of view. But Megan was determined not to join in. 'I'm tired,' she said with a shrug of her shoulders. 'Think I'll have a bath and an early night.'

She left the room and went upstairs. She would leave them to it.

As soon as John heard the sound of water filling the bath, he got up and switched off the television. 'Go on like this, Anne, and you'll push her too hard,' he said. 'She'll get fed up with it.'

'I'm not pushing her too hard,' Anne snapped back. 'She loves her sport.'

'I know, but you've got to let her be a normal teenager as well as a star athlete.'

'What, let her hang around the town centre, or in the burger bar? Is that what you mean?'

'If that's what she wants to do, sometimes, then yes, that's fine.' Their voices were getting louder. John went to the sofa and sat close to Anne. 'It's what kids do,' he said more quietly. 'I did it, you did it, it's the sort of thing that everyone does when they're young.'

Anne frowned. 'Her new friend, Katy, is coming to stay next Saturday. You know, the one she met at the training weekend?'

'And I suppose they'll just talk about athletics all weekend. Or go training together. There have to be other things in life.'

'The trouble with you is that you never take anything seriously.'

John sighed. 'Look, Anne, you were a terrific athlete. I know, because if you remember, I used to come and watch you, almost every weekend. And I know how much you loved it. But ... but you never quite achieved what you thought you should have achieved, did you? And now...' His voice trailed away.

'And now...?'

'Well it ... it seems to me that you're trying to realise your dreams through Megan. It's like, for you, if she makes it to the top then you will have made it after all.'

Anne stared at her husband for a few moments, not saying anything. Then her eyes moistened and a tear ran down one cheek. She got up from the sofa and walked from the room.

John sighed. 'Oh, brilliant, John,' he said out loud. 'You handled that really well. Brilliant.'

# Seven

For the next few days the atmosphere in the house was strained and tense. Anne and John hardly spoke to each other and several times Megan thought about calling Katy and putting off her visit.

But she was really looking forward to seeing her new friend, and not only because they had a shared love of athletics. They got on really well, too.

On Wednesday evening, when Megan and Anne got home from training, they went in through the kitchen door as usual, and saw a large bunch of white roses sitting on the kitchen table. They were wrapped in clear cellophane and tied with a ribbon.

Megan smiled at her mum. 'Wonder who they're from?'

Anne went to the flowers and freed a small envelope from the cellophane. Inside was card with a handwritten message. She read it out loud. '"I'm very sorry. I love you."' She looked at Megan. 'And there are three kisses.'

Megan smiled. 'They are beautiful, Mum,'

'I'd better put them into water,' said Anne. She went to a cupboard and took out a vase. As she was unwrapping the flowers, the door to the living room opened and John stood there, almost as though he was scared to come all the way into the room.

'They're lovely. Thank you,' Anne said, not really looking at her husband. She placed the twelve roses into the vase and began arranging them.

'White roses are your favourites, right?' John said from the doorway.

Megan decided that it was probably a good idea to make herself scarce. 'Better start my homework,' she said. 'Give me a call when tea's ready, eh?' She smiled at her mum and then squeezed past her dad in the doorway, silently mouthing, 'Good luck,' as she went by.

John stepped into the room and closed the door. He leaned against it for a moment and then moved to the table, watching Anne arrange the flowers. 'I'm sorry,' he said at last. 'I shouldn't have said what I did.'

Anne shrugged her shoulders but continued looking

at the flowers. 'Maybe you're right. Maybe I am pushing her too hard.'

'You're only doing what you think is best for Megan.'

Anne finally raised her eyes from the flowers and she looked directly at him. 'That's not what you said the other day.'

'But I didn't mean…'

'No, I've thought about it a lot and I'll try not to be quite so intense about training; I'll be a bit more relaxed.'

'And I'll try, too,' John said.

'To do what?'

'To, er … to er…' He smiled. 'To be even more perfect?'

Anne laughed as the tension in the room drained away. She went over to the sink to put water into the vase. 'They really are gorgeous,' she said.

When Megan came down a little later, her parents were chatting as though there had been no row at all. 'Everything okay?' she asked.

'Perfect,' her dad said. 'Like your mum.'

Anne raised her eyebrows and smiled. 'Like those beautiful roses, maybe.'

'Well, you're perfect for me,' John said. He went over to Anne, put his arms around her and gave her a kiss.'

'Oh, please,' Megan said, pulling a face, 'that is so gross!' But really, she was delighted that her parents were happy again.

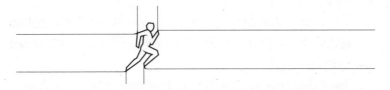

When Katy arrived for her visit on Saturday morning the upset in the Morgan house had been forgotten. The only reminders were the twelve white roses, which still looked lovely.

Megan and her parents collected Katy from the train station and after lunch, the girls were dropped off in the town centre. Megan still had some birthday money – a present from one set of grandparents – and she wanted to spend it on a new pair of shoes.

'I saw them ages ago,' she said to Katy as they looked at the shoes on display in the shop window.'

'They're really nice,' Katy said. 'Let's see if they've got your size.'

Megan was in luck. Ten minutes later the girls emerged from the shop with Megan clutching a carrier bag containing her new pair of shoes.

As they walked along the street, chatting happily, it suddenly began to rain, quite heavily. The girls were both wearing summer clothes, so they made a run for a little café Megan sometimes went to with her friends.

They got themselves drinks and were sitting chatting when the door to the café opened and three boys walked in.

'Oh, no,' Megan groaned.

Katy glanced at the boys and then back at Megan. 'What's wrong?'

'See the one at the front, the one making all the noise? His name's Gavin Richards. He goes to my school. They all do. Gavin thinks he's a bit special, but he's actually very boring.'

Katy shrugged. 'We'll ignore them.'

But ignoring the boys wasn't as simple as Katy thought it would be. Once they spotted Megan, and as soon as they'd bought their drinks, they came over and sat at the table immediately next to the girls.

'All right, Meg?' Gavin Richards said. He pointed to the shoe-shop bag at Megan's feet. 'You got some new shoes, then?'

'Yes, thanks,' Megan said, trying to keep the conversation between them as brief as possible.

'What, running shoes are they? Or trainers?'

Gavin's two friends nudged each other with their

elbows and almost choked on their drinks. They seemed to think his comment was hilarious.

But Megan shook her head. 'If you must know, no, they're not.'

'Oh,' Gavin said, grinning at his friends. 'Thought that was all you did. Like, running, or training.'

'Grow up, Gavin,' said Megan, who was starting to feel cross.

Gavin didn't look as if he was in a hurry to grow up. He seemed more interested in impressing his mates. He looked at Katy. 'Who's this, then? Another runner?'

Katy ignored him.

'Can't she speak, Meg? Can't she say nothing?'

'I can speak perfectly well, thanks,' Katy said. 'Better than you can, by the sound of it.'

Gavin's eyes widened at the sound of Katy's voice and her strong Liverpool accent. 'A Scouser!' he said. 'Which team do you support? Liverpool or Everton?'

'There's only one team in Liverpool, isn't there?' Katy answered. 'Liverpool, of course.'

'Yes!' Gavin and his friends said together, giving each other high fives. Gavin turned back to Katy. 'Respect! You know what, you sound just like Stevie Gerrard.'

'Oh, great. Thanks very much.'

'No, it's a compliment,' Gavin said very seriously. 'Stevie G's my hero.'

From then on, Gavin and his friends virtually ignored Megan as they talked football with the honoured visitor from Liverpool. Soon, though, Megan noticed that the rain had stopped and the girls left the café, saying they had to meet her parents.

'Do you really support Liverpool?' Megan asked as they walked towards the bus stop.

'I don't support any team,' said Katy. 'I don't really like football.'

'But you sounded as if you knew so much about it when you were talking…'

'When you've got two brothers and you go to my school, Stevie G and Liverpool is all you ever hear about.'

'But how did you know which team to pick when he asked?'

Katy laughed. 'Didn't you see what he was wearing under his jacket?'

Megan smiled as she remembered. 'Oh, yes. A red Liverpool shirt.'

A bus was approaching and Megan pointed towards it. 'That's ours. Race you to the bus stop.'

That evening the girls went tenpin bowling with

Megan's parents. John, as usual, played it all for fun, even though he was a very good bowler. The girls and Anne played a little more seriously. Soon they were all having a great time.

With three frames to go, John was in the lead. It was his turn. He stood at the end of the aisle and took aim, with the bowling ball up at his chest. 'Watch this and learn, girls,' he said, looking back at the others.

'Just get on with it, Dad.' Megan laughed.

John began his run up. The ball swung smoothly back and then forward and at the moment of release it thudded heavily down onto the wooden lane. After just a few metres it lurched off course, crashed into the gully and continued on its way, leaving the pins completely undisturbed.

Megan and Katy burst into laughter, but Anne looked cross. 'John, you did that on purpose.'

'No, I didn't,' John said, lifting up both hands to protest his innocence.

'You did. You never miss completely.'

'Even geniuses get it wrong, sometimes.' He looked at Megan and Katy. 'Don't they, girls?'

The two girls grinned, enjoying the joke.

But Anne wasn't happy. 'You're just trying to let someone else win.'

John shrugged. 'So I did it on purpose. What's the problem? I don't care about winning.'

'Well, you should, sometimes.

'But why?'

'None of us wants you to let us win. Winning's no fun that way. And what sort of example is it to the girls, being happy to lose like that? They're athletes. They want to win fairly.'

Megan glanced at her friend, who looked a little embarrassed.

John's ball rolled out of the return tunnel. He picked it up and turned for his second attempt. He moved smoothly again and this time the ball was softer onto the wood as he released it. It streaked up the lane, a fraction off centre, smashed into the pins and all ten went flying.

A strike!

Katy was lying on a camp bed in Megan's room. It was late and the girls had been chatting quietly, not wanting to disturb Megan's parents.

Katy was doing most of the chatting. She said that she noticed since the bowling alley that her friend had seemed a little down. Now though, they had both been silent for a few minutes.

'Are you still awake?' Katy whispered.

'Yes.'

'What are you thinking about?'

Megan thought for a few moments. 'Just … stuff, I guess.'

'What stuff?'

'Like today. Those boys.'

'What about them?'

Megan sighed. 'Just because I'm good at running, they think that running is the only thing in my life. And just because I've got a bag from a shoe shop, they think I've bought running shoes or trainers.'

'They're jealous. You've got a special talent, and they haven't.'

Megan had obviously been doing a lot of thinking. 'Then tonight, at the bowling alley.'

'It was great. I really enjoyed it.'

'Yeah, but … Mum and Dad…'

'They're nice, too.'

'I know, but that stuff about winning and losing, it was embarrassing. Sometimes I wish that not everything was about running all the time, especially with my parents. It's almost all we ever talk about.'

Katy sat up in her bed. 'You're lucky, Meg. Both of your parents care about you, really care. I hardly ever see my dad; a few times a year, maybe, when he can be bothered.

Megan knew that Katy's parents were divorced and

that she lived with her mum and two younger brothers. She suddenly felt very guilty about her own complaints.

'You're right,' she said. 'I am lucky, and I shouldn't moan.'

It had been a long day and Katy was unable to stop herself from yawning. 'It's okay,' she said. 'Everyone needs to moan to their friends sometimes.' She settled down under her duvet. 'We'd better go to sleep or I'll never get up in the morning. Goodnight.'

'Goodnight,' Megan replied.

She lay back on her pillow, her eyes still open. Through a gap in the curtains she could see the darkness of the night outside. She closed her eyes, her mind still racing, and it was a long time before she finally fell asleep.

# Eight

Megan's win in the county championships had not only produced a record-breaking run, it had also won her a place in the national schools' championships. It was a tremendous achievement considering that it had been her first county competition.

But the national championship was a huge step up, and as Megan was running in the under-15s 100 metres, it meant again that there would be girls nearly a year older than her in the same event. And this time she would be up against runners from all over the country.

It was a windy, cold and cloudy day; summer seemed to have forgotten that it was summer. The athletes were all wearing tracksuits as they warmed up for their events; no one wanted to risk a pulled muscle. Most of the spectators were dressed in clothes more suited to winter, and the few braver ones who had stuck to shorts and T-shirts could be seen shivering as the biting wind cut across the stadium.

The weather didn't suit fast times for the sprint races, especially as the wind was blowing directly into the faces of the runners as they battled their way up the finishing straight.

As Megan watched the first few races, she noticed that the blustery conditions seemed to be causing false starts. Runners were struggling to settle properly as they got into the 'set' position.

'You'll have to be careful of that,' her mum said when Megan mentioned it. 'We don't want to come all this way and then be disqualified for a false start.'

There was something else playing on Megan's mind as she completed her warm-up; she had only recently begun to use starting blocks and wasn't finding it easy. She mentioned it to Anne.

'Do you want to start without blocks?' her mum said. 'You don't have to use them.'

'No,' Megan answered firmly. 'I've got to get used to them. I'll be fine.'

The crowd suddenly burst into cheers of encouragement followed by applause as another group of young sprinters hurtled up the straight and crossed the line in a tight finish.

Megan's race was next. She hugged her mum, who whispered, 'Good luck.'

'Thanks,' Megan said.

'Remember: fast away, relax into your running and

keep your form all the way to the line,' Anne called as Megan walked away to join the other girls at the start.

Megan nodded, thinking that racing wasn't just about running. There was so much more to get right.

A few minutes later, the eight competitors were ready for the race. Megan had been drawn in lane eight, the furthest from the starter. It wasn't her favourite lane, but there was nothing she could do. She just had to get on with it.

The girls were ready, some of them shivering slightly in the blustery wind. Suddenly rain began to fall. It wasn't heavy, but Megan saw umbrellas going up all around the stadium.

Wind, lane eight and now rain; Megan began to think that everything was against her.

The starter's voice told the girls to get to their marks.

The track had already turned dark and shiny as the rain fell steadily. Megan wiped raindrops from her eyes and walked forward. She crouched down, placed the soles of both feet against her starting blocks and settled into position. The blocks were meant to help Megan push away at the start of her race, and when she got it right, they did. But with the soles of her feet against the blocks and her toes still touching the ground, she sometimes felt a little unbalanced as she rose into the 'set' position. It had caused her to stumble several times in training, but she pushed that from her mind as she waited.

'Set.'

The girls rose and tried to keep still as the wind gusted and the rain soaked through their vests and onto their skin.

A tiny movement to Megan's left caused first one, then another and then all eight girls to burst from the line, before the starter's gun had even sounded.

A false start!

The runners looked anxiously at each other as they walked back down their lanes. No one liked a false start; it made the nerves jangle. And another one could mean a runner being disqualified.

'On your marks.'

The girls took their starting positions for a second time.

'Set!'

They rose in their blocks.

And waited.

Perhaps it was the fear of causing another false start, perhaps it was the slight worry about the blocks, perhaps it was the wind and the rain or perhaps it was being in lane eight. But when the pistol sounded, Megan hesitated for a moment. And in a 100-metres race, a moment's hesitation can mean the difference between winning and losing.

Megan was the last girl away from the start and after the first ten metres she was easily in last position. She knew it. And she knew that Anne would know it, too.

Megan tried to battle her way back into the race, all the way up the straight. She passed two girls quickly and by the 30-metres mark had passed a third. She was in her full stride after ten more metres and closing on the next girl. It was tight, all the girls were sprinting hard and fighting against the wind and the rain.

Megan passed one more girl; she was in fourth place. But then before she knew it the finish line was just metres ahead. All the leading girls dipped forward as they crossed the line, but Megan knew instantly that she had finished out of the top positions, in fourth place.

She felt disappointed and furious with herself for messing up her start. A good start and it might have been so different. She turned to congratulate the winner and the other girls in the race and then trudged off the track to where her mum was waiting.

'I messed it up,' Megan said quickly, before Anne could speak.

Anne remained silent, seeming unsure of what to say.

'The start,' Megan said, almost to herself. 'I got it all wrong. Everything.'

'Never mind,' Anne replied at last. 'You ran well, once you got going. And it's all a learning curve.'

Megan suddenly felt a little tearful, not because she'd lost, but because she felt that she hadn't done as well as she could.

She glanced at her mum, at that moment wanting a comforting hug more than any words. But it didn't come.

Anne smiled at her daughter but she couldn't keep the disappointment she felt from showing on her face.

# Nine

The school year was over, but high summer meant that the athletics season was still in full swing.

Most of Megan's school friends had gone on holiday, some abroad, some to the nearby coastal parts of Wales, some staying with friends or relatives. Ellie and Beth were in Spain.

Ellie had been talking about her family holiday to Spain for months; her parents had booked a villa in a holiday village on the coast for a whole three weeks.

And then, just before the end of term, Ellie's older brother decided that he wanted to stay at home to earn some extra cash for when he started at university. So Ellie's parents told her that she could invite a friend to join them on the trip. When Ellie said that she couldn't possibly choose between Beth and Megan, her parents said she could invite them both, as all three girls could share a room.

Ellie was so excited when she asked Megan and Beth to join her. Being Ellie, she'd already planned out most of the holiday they would all enjoy. There would be endless sunshine, golden beaches, a glittering sea, delicious and exotic food – which was always very important for Ellie – and dancing every night.

Megan and Beth were thrilled at the offer, and both said they would have to speak to their parents about it.

But before Megan even reached home, she'd made up her own mind that she wouldn't go. She'd got over the disappointment of her run at the national championships, but it had made her even more determined to make a success of the rest of the season. Three weeks in sunny Spain with her two best school friends would be fantastic, but it would also mean missing so much training and some important races.

When Megan got home she told her mum about Ellie's holiday invitation. Anne listened patiently and then said that if Megan really wanted to go on the trip then she could, as she knew it would be a special holiday.

But Megan really had decided not to go, and she could see that her mum was quite relieved when she told her and explained why. Anne nodded and said, 'Well, all athletes have to make some sacrifices if they want to make it to the very top.'

And that was it. Megan didn't bother to talk about it with her dad; she knew he'd try to push her into going. She was pleased she'd made the decision for herself and she was going to stick with it.

At school the next day, Ellie and Beth were

disappointed when Megan said that she wouldn't be joining them on the holiday. They said that they understood, but for the last couple of weeks of term, Megan felt a little left out when her friends talked about the fun they were going to have in Spain and then practised their few Spanish phrases on each other.

Since they'd left for their holiday, Megan had received a couple of texts from both girls. But at the end of the second week, a postcard addressed to Megan came through the letterbox.

Megan's dad happened to pick up the post. He looked at the postcard with its split pictures of a beautiful, sunlit beach and the holiday village at night, and then turned it over. He saw that it was addressed to Megan but couldn't stop himself from reading Ellie's scratchy writing:

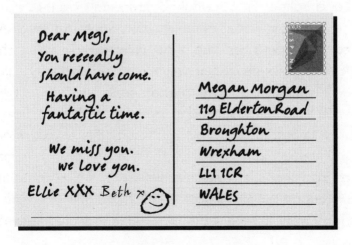

Dear Megs,
You reeeeally should have come.
Having a fantastic time.

We miss you.
we love you.
Ellie XXX Beth x

Megan Morgan
119 Elderton Road
Broughton
Wrexham
LL1 1CR
WALES

John frowned and read the postcard again before going through to the kitchen where Megan and her mum were sitting having breakfast. 'Postcard for you,' he said, dropping the card in front of Megan.

Megan read the card quickly, smiled and passed it to her mum.

'Sounds lovely,' Anne said and continued with her breakfast.

John poured himself a cup of tea and looked at Anne and Megan in turn. No one spoke. He sipped his tea and put down the cup. 'Anyone have anything to tell me?'

'Like what?' Anne said, raising her eyebrows.

John sighed. 'Like, the fact that Megan was invited on a holiday and no one bothered mentioning it to me?'

Megan and her mum exchanged guilty looks.

'I was invited,' Megan said. 'But I didn't want to go.'

'A holiday in Spain! And you didn't want to go?' He looked at Anne. 'Is this down to you? Did you stop her from going because of her running?'

'No!' Megan and her mum said together.

'It was my decision,' Megan added.

'But you'd have had a great time. You've never been to Spain.'

'I will go, one day.'

John shook his head. 'Athletics!'

Megan got to her feet. 'Dad, I love athletics. And I didn't want to miss a big part of the season. I know it would have been great, but there'll be other times.'

John looked at Anne. 'But you knew about this?'

Anne nodded and John turned back to Megan. 'You told your mum all about it, but not me. Why was that?'

'Because ... because I knew you'd have tried to make me go.'

'Oh, you think so, do you?' John said. 'Well, as it happens, I wouldn't have done anything of the sort. I would have respected your decision.' He looked very disappointed. 'But it would have been nice to have been told about it in the first place.'

The following weekend, Megan did well in two junior events in a club meet, winning the 100-metres race and finishing second in the sprint hurdles race. Her dad congratulated her when she got home, but not as enthusiastically as usual. He had been very quiet since the upset over the holiday. There had been few smiles or jokes in the Morgan home.

During the next week, Megan trained each evening with her mum. But on the Friday afternoon, as she was getting ready to go to meet Anne at the athletics track, her dad surprisingly turned up at home.

'Get your coat and let's go,' he said to Megan with a big smile on his face.

'Go? Where?' answered a surprised Megan. 'Are you taking me to training?'

'You're not training tonight. I'm taking you to see Liverpool play the mighty Barcelona.'

The full football season was yet to start, but the clubs were already playing pre-season friendly games. And big clubs like Liverpool were playing against top European teams.

'But ... I thought you were going with your friend from work?'

'He can't make it after all,' John said, smiling. 'There's no point in wasting a ticket is there? And as you decided not to go with Ellie and Beth, watching a Spanish team is as close as you'll get to Spain this summer.'

'But ... but what about training?'

'You can miss training for once. Now, come on, hurry up. Chances like this don't come along very often. Some of the best players in Europe and a whole bunch of World Cup winners will be out there tonight.'

'But ... but...'

'No more buts. Go and get what you need and we're off.'

'But what about Mum?'

John laughed. 'I said no more buts. I'll sort it with your mum. Now hurry up, we've got a long drive.'

# Ten

Liverpool's Anfield stadium was packed for the visit of such a special team, and from the kick-off both teams showed they wanted to win, even though it was only a friendly match.

Megan and John sat high up in one of the stands. As she watched, Megan was thinking how good it was to be out with her dad – he could be such fun. Like the thousands of other fans all around them, they joined in the chanting, and cheered and applauded and shouted, especially when the Liverpool players were attacking the Barcelona goal.

After twenty minutes Liverpool scored the opening goal. Megan jumped to her feet and yelled in delight, realising that when she got back to school after the holiday, this would be something to show off about. Gavin Richards and his friends would be so impressed. She decided she'd take in the match programme to show them.

Barcelona equalised soon after and at half-time the scores were level. While Megan sipped a soft drink, her dad was busy exchanging texts with someone. In the rush to leave home, Megan had left her own mobile phone in her bedroom, but her dad was already typing out his third text since the half-time whistle had sounded.

'Who are you texting?' Megan asked.

'Your mum,' John said as he pressed the send button on his phone.

'Everything okay?'

'Fine.'

'You did sort it with Mum, didn't you? You did call her?'

'I couldn't get through. I sent her a text.'

'Dad!' Megan suddenly felt anxious. 'Is she angry about me coming?'

'It'll be fine. Don't worry. Look, the players are coming out again.'

The crowd roared as the two teams emerged from the tunnel and walked back onto the pitch. Once the second half was underway, the match continued to be a close contest. Liverpool grabbed the lead for the second time and held on to it until the ninety minutes were almost up.

But then, with just five minutes to go, Barcelona scored a spectacular equalising goal. All around the ground there were groans from the Liverpool supporters, but John applauded loudly. 'Great goal,' he said, nodding his approval. 'Brilliant.'

A few Liverpool supporters sitting nearby glared at John, and one man a few rows back called out to him, 'We're Liverpool supporters here, pal, not Barcelona.'

John just smiled. 'I support football,' he said to Megan. 'And that was a great goal.'

Soon after, the referee blew the final whistle and the match ended in a two-two draw. 'Fair result,' John said as he and Megan joined the thousands of supporters making their way towards the exits. 'Great game, though.'

'Do you really not care about winning, Dad?' Megan asked. 'Not even with Liverpool?'

They were walking down the first flight of steps towards the exit and John held on to his daughter's hand to make sure he didn't lose her amongst the crowd. 'I prefer it if they win, of course,' he said. 'But if they lose it doesn't really matter, does it? Sport's like that – no one and no team can win all the time. If they did it would be boring.'

Megan thought about what her dad had said as they walked back to the car. It took a long time to reach it and even longer to get out of the Liverpool area and onto the road back towards Wrexham.

Traffic was very heavy and a journey that should have taken around an hour took more than two. It was very late, well after midnight, when John finally pulled the car onto the drive.

The kitchen light was still burning and as Megan and her dad walked wearily through the door they saw Anne sitting at the table.

Her face was like thunder.

For a few moments no one said a thing. Anne and John simply stared at each other. But when John went to speak, Anne got in first and the argument started. 'I know why you did this,' she said furiously, her eyes blazing. 'It was to spite me, wasn't it?'

'Oh, don't be ridiculous!' John snapped back. 'That's just stupid! Crazy!'

Megan had never seen or heard her parents so angry with each other.

'And you should have called me instead of just sending a text!' Anne yelled. 'Why didn't you call me?'

Megan stared at her dad, remembering that he'd told her he had tried to call Anne but couldn't get through. It wasn't true; he hadn't even tried to call.

'I didn't call because I knew that if I did you'd complain again and try to stop us from going!' John shouted back. 'You'd want to stop us from enjoying ourselves. Like you always do. Every time!'

It was as though Anne hadn't heard a word. 'She should never be out this late on a night before a race!' she almost screamed, pointing at Megan. 'She's supposed to be running for the club tomorrow.' She glanced up at the clock on the wall. 'Today! There's absolutely no point in her even turning up to race now. She'll be exhausted!'

Megan looked at the clock and saw that it was almost twenty to one in the morning. 'Mum, I'll be...'

'You be quiet, Megan,' Anne snarled. 'I'm cross with you, as well. Staying out this late the night before you're meant to run...'

'It's not Megan's fault,' John snapped. 'Don't start blaming her.'

'I blame both of you! You should both have known better!'

'But I'll be okay to run, Mum.'

'There's no way you're running. You'll be in no fit state and it'll be embarrassing for both of us.'

'But...'

'Is that what you're really worried about, Anne?' John said. 'Being embarrassed?'

Anne glared at Megan. 'Go to bed,' she said quietly. 'We'll talk about this tomorrow.'

Megan knew that there was no point in arguing, and anyway, she suddenly felt very tired. She trudged wearily up the stairs and went into the bathroom. By the time she was ready for bed she could still hear raised voices coming from the kitchen.

She closed her bedroom door, got into bed and pulled the duvet over her head.

# Eleven

The next training weekend was just a week away, but the days dragged on and on because of the tension at home. Finally though, the weekend arrived and Megan felt relieved to be away from the house, even for just one night.

There were fewer young athletes taking part this time as some were away with their families on summer holidays. Fortunately for Megan, her friend Katy was there, and that helped her unwind and start to enjoy herself again.

On the Sunday morning, Carole the coach worked on the track with the group of young sprinters, including Megan and Katy.

They were doing a training exercise that involved repeated, long-striding runs over fifty or sixty metres before slowing and walking until Carole gave them the signal to run again. The young sprinters breathed hard, waiting for Carole's command to begin the next run.

'And … go!'

Five sprinters began to run. One didn't. It was Megan.

Carole came over. 'Megan, are you okay?' she said. 'You don't seem completely focused today.'

'I … I'm…

'Are you injured?'

'No. I … I … I'm sorry.' Megan's face turned very red. 'I wasn't concentrating.'

Carole nodded and smiled, but didn't say more. The other runners were still on their long-striding runs.

'And … slow into walk!' Carole called. She watched as the young sprinters gradually slowed to walking-pace. 'Okay everyone, we'll take a little break,' she told them.

Megan was sitting on the grass at the trackside, gazing into space, when she heard footsteps approaching. She looked up and saw Carole coming towards her.

'Want to talk?' Carole said with a smile. She sat next to Megan.

Megan hesitated. She felt confused, with terribly mixed emotions. She loved both her parents and was always loyal to them. Talking about them and their recent arguments to another adult, even a kind and supportive adult like Carole, felt wrong. 'No,' she said at last. 'I'm fine, thanks.'

'Are you sure? Everything okay at home now with your mum and dad?'

Megan's heart was thumping in her chest. She stared across the track, not wanting to catch Carole's eye. 'Yes, everything's fine,' she said. But she felt uncomfortable about not telling the truth.

Carole smiled and got to her feet. 'Okay. But you know I'm not just here to help you run faster, don't you? Come and find me if you do want to have a chat. About anything.'

Megan nodded. 'I will. Thank you.'

As she watched Carole walk away, Megan was tempted to call her back and try to explain exactly what was playing on her mind. But she didn't. How could she possibly explain that the relief at being away from home that she'd felt the previous day was quickly disappearing? And how could she tell her that the thought of returning to arguing parents made her gloomy and sad? It was all too embarrassing and upsetting.

On the other side of the track, Katy was talking to a few of the other young athletes. Megan could see her laughing. Her friend looked carefree and happy, but then she always did.

Megan sat wondering why Katy always managed

to look so cheerful. Katy's life was far less easy than Megan's. Her mum worked and she spent a lot of time helping out at home. And because her dad wasn't around, money was always tight.

Megan had no such problems. Her mum and dad both had good jobs and were loving and supportive. At home, she tidied her own room when her mum reminded her and sometimes helped a bit in the kitchen, but that was about it. She suddenly felt guilty about feeling sorry for herself and quickly got to her feet, determined to cheer up. And for the rest of the morning, training went much more smoothly.

Towards the end of the lunch break, Megan's mobile phone began to ring. She picked it up and saw that her mum was calling.

'Hi, Mum?'

'Hello, darling. How are you?'

'Fine. Why are you calling? I'll be seeing you in a few hours.'

'I just thought I'd check that you're okay. I knew this might be a good time to catch you.'

'I can't speak for long.'

'Are you working hard?'

' 'Course I am. I always do.'

'Are you racing?'

'No, just training. We're having some fun relays later, like last time.'

Anne's next words cut into Megan like a knife. 'Well, make sure you win, like last time. You've got to keep that winning streak going.'

Megan could feel the tension building inside her.

'I'm sure you'll tell me you won when I collect you,' Anne added.

'They're no big deal, Mum,' Megan said sharply. 'Look, I've got to go now. See you later. Bye.'

'Bye, love, see you…'

Megan didn't hear the final words her mum spoke. She had already ended the call.

By the time the relay races came around, Megan was anxious and nervy. She and Katy were in the same team, like before, but this time the quartet was made up by two different girls.

Megan was running the third leg again and, just like last time, she would be handing the baton on to Katy. She stood in her lane and looked over to the other side of the track as the race began. The two new team mates seemed to be even stronger runners than the original pair, because as the girl running the second leg approached Megan she was clearly in the lead.

Megan waited and then, arm stretched back for the baton, she began her run. She must have set off a little late because before she had taken many strides her team mate was almost up alongside her. She tried to pass the baton but it missed Megan's hand. The girl slowed quickly – too quickly – and Megan made another grab for the baton. She got it, somehow, but it was a terrible change over, and as Megan sprinted on and leaned into the bend, she saw that she had lost at least one place, possibly two.

She pounded round the bend and glimpsed Katy glancing back at her, before starting her own run, arm stretched back.

At the change over, the track was very crowded, with all the teams neck and neck.

Megan reached forward with the baton, stretching towards her friend's open hand. The baton brushed Katy's fingers and then, for some reason she couldn't understand or even begin to explain, Megan let go of the smooth cylinder. It was a fraction of a second too soon and there was nothing Katy could do to take the baton safely.

Horrified, Megan watched it fall and bounce onto the track as the other runners sped away towards the finish line.

Katy slowed and stopped and then turned back, and Megan feared that her friend might be furious. It had been Megan's mistake, no doubt about it.

But Katy was smiling. 'We made a real mess of that, didn't we?' she laughed, jogging back to Megan.

'You didn't; it was me. I'm so sorry, Katy.' Megan was close to tears.

Katy put her arm around her friend. 'Hey, it doesn't

matter, she said. 'It was only for fun. And anyway, it happens all the time, even with proper teams. Don't worry about it, Meg.'

But Megan was worried. She felt that she'd let her team mates down and she could already imagine the comments her mum would make when she learned about the dropped baton. She trudged off the track, feeling pretty miserable as the weekend session came to an end.

Carole stopped Megan as she went to pass her on the way to the changing rooms. 'Megan, can I have a quick word?' the coach said.

'I'm sorry,' Megan said before Carole had the chance to continue. 'It was a terrible change over and it was all my fault. I dropped the baton, not Katy...'

'Megan,' Carole said firmly, 'dropping the baton doesn't matter, you know that. The races are just meant as a bit of light relief at the end of the session.'

'Yes, but...'

'Listen to me,' Carole said kindly. 'The important thing, whenever and wherever you run, is that you enjoy it. Try to remember that, Megan. There's no point in running if you don't enjoy it.'

# Twelve

'So you really don't mind?' said Carole. The coach held the phone tightly as she waited for Anne's answer.

Carole had been worried about Megan at the training weekend – she hadn't looked at all happy – and had decided to telephone her mum to find out what was wrong. A chat would do no harm and might even help. But Anne kept the discussion firmly on athletics, telling Carole that Megan was training and running well and enjoying it as much as ever.

The coach soon realised that there was no way she was going to find out anything on the phone. It was when Anne mentioned Megan's next competition that Carole saw her opportunity – and grabbed it. If she went to see Megan run, it would be the perfect way for the coach to see for herself just how much the girl was enjoying her athletics.

'I'd be delighted if you watched her race,' replied Anne. 'And I'm sure Megan would love it too. She's always saying how much she enjoys your coaching.'

'That's good to hear,' said Carole.

'It's the annual match between clubs from our part of the country,' Anne told her. 'It's always exciting; I ran in it myself years ago. And Megan is actually going for three events this time.'

'Really?' Carole said.

'She wants to give it a try,' said Anne. 'It could be the first step on the road to the heptathlon.'

'Mmm, it could be,' replied the coach. 'I'll look forward to it.'

'I'll email the details and see you there,' said Anne.

After the call, Carole was thoughtful. She was beginning to think that she might know what was wrong with Megan...

Megan was thrilled when Anne said that Carole would be at the event. It would be a good chance to show the coach that she was feeling much better. This was partly because for the past couple of weeks her parents had stopped arguing and were not only talking to each other, but actually smiling and laughing again.

And Megan had also taken Carole's words about enjoying her athletics to heart. She knew the coach was totally right. And when Megan thought it through, she realised that she'd been letting her worries get in the way of the thing she loved most of all: running.

So she made a vow to stop worrying and to enjoy her sport. And she really was enjoying it. Training had been excellent and fun, and she was looking forward to trying three events in one day for the very first time.

It would be tough, but Megan was up for it.

The weather was lovely on the day of Megan's attempt at three different events. There was a bright blue sky dotted with a few fluffy clouds and a light breeze, just enough to stop the summer heat from becoming too fierce. Most of the crowd wore T-shirts and shorts. Ice-cream vans and cold-drink sellers were doing good business.

The day was almost perfect, for athletes and spectators alike. And it turned out to be almost perfect for Megan Morgan.

From the moment she got up she felt good, fitter and stronger than ever. She'd slept well and her eyes were bright and shiny when she stared into the bathroom mirror, grinning back at herself as she brushed her teeth.

She bounced down the stairs for breakfast and then

chatted happily to her mum on the way to the track, with no sign of the nerves she had been feeling over the previous weeks.

The stadium was already filling with athletes and spectators when she saw Carole. The coach found Megan and her mum for a few quick words before the meet began.

Carole was pleased to see that, just as Anne had told her, Megan seemed to be back to her old, happy self. They chatted for a while and then Megan jogged off to begin her warm-up and prepare for her first event of the day, the 100 metres.

And when it came, it was almost no contest. This time Megan got her start absolutely right, exploding from the blocks with no problems and then leading the race from start to finish. She crossed the line nearly three metres ahead of the second-placed runner.

In the crowd, Carole smiled and nodded her approval as she checked the stopwatch she had used to time Megan's run. If the official timing was the same, Megan certainly was back to her best – better than her best.

There was hardly time to snatch a breather because the long-jump competition started soon after.

Before Megan's first jump, she paced out her run-up very carefully. Like the other competitors, she placed a marker next to the runway. This was to show her that the distance from the marker to the take-off board was exactly the right length for the number of strides she had practised over and over again in training, to get the take-off exactly right.

If Megan got it right, her foot would thump down close to the front edge of the board for the jump. But it couldn't be over the front edge – that meant a 'no jump', which would not count in the competition.

Megan got it right.

When it was her turn she went to the end of the runway and stood, leaning slightly forward, with both hands resting on one knee. She had got into the habit of taking up this position before each jump.

She stared down the runway to the pit, concentrating hard and focusing on her jump. Then she took a deep breath, rocked gently backward and forward three times and launched herself into her run-up. She passed her marker and – exactly the correct number of strides later – her foot thumped down on to the board. Megan soared into the air, kicked and then stretched her arms and legs forward and landed in the pit, sending the soft sand flying.

It was good, very good, and the spectators near the long-jump pit, including her mum and Carole, applauded loudly. Megan scrambled to her feet, smiling and knowing before her jump was even measured that she had gone into first place.

Her second-round jump was even better and she increased her lead over the second-placed girl.

In the third round, feeling on top of the world, she leapt further still. But she had tried just a little too hard on her run-up. As her foot hit the take-off board it was just a little too far forward, pressing into the Plasticine at the front edge, leaving a clear mark in it as she jumped. It was a 'no jump', the only blip in what had been, so far, a perfect day.

But it didn't matter; no one else got close to Megan's longest jump.

After two wins from two events, now only the 75-metres hurdles race remained. Could it possibly be three out of three?

# Thirteen

There was quite a wait before the hurdles race, so Carole took the opportunity to slip away from trackside to talk about Megan's progress with the head coach of her club. His name was Danny and he was bubbling with enthusiasm for the club's star athlete. 'She's doing tremendously well, as you can see from today. We're all very proud of her. We think she can go all the way to the top.'

It all sounded good, but Carole wanted to know more. 'And Anne's coaching methods seem to be working well?'

Danny hesitated before replying. 'Anne is certainly a terrific coach,' he said at last.

Carole sensed that he was reluctant to say more. It was important that she learned all the facts, though.

'But...?' she said. 'And there is a but, isn't there?'

Over on the track, a 1500-metres race was taking place and a tightly bunched group of runners picked up the pace in the final lap of their race, preparing for the sprint finish. Danny watched them go by before speaking again. 'I've known Anne for years. We're old friends,' he said. 'When she was hurdling for the club, I was sprinting. Anne was always a great competitor and she's a great coach, too.'

'All sounds good so far,' Carole said, encouraging Danny to continue.

'We've got a lot of very promising young sprinters and hurdlers,' Danny went on. 'It's probably the strongest section of our club. I coach them and it's a big job. I reckon some of them could really benefit from working with Anne.'

'That sounds like a great idea.'

'Yeah,' Danny said. 'But unfortunately, Anne's not interested in anyone else. She's only interested in Megan. I'm afraid it's a bit of an...' He stopped again.

'What?' Carole asked.

'Well, to be truthful ... a bit of an obsession.'

Carole nodded. It was just as she'd thought.

'And there's another thing,' Danny said.

'What's that?' Carole asked. It appeared, after all, that Danny had quite a lot he wanted to say.

'Well, you're a coach,' Danny said. 'You know what it's like. We all have coaching ideas; different techniques we think could help an athlete. I'd like the chance to work with Megan, because I think I could help her run even faster.'

The 1500-metres race had finished and officials were placing hurdles across the track for Megan's final event when Carole made her way back towards the finish line. She was deep in thought.

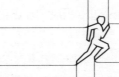

The sprint hurdles had been Anne's event when she competed, so she was really keen for Megan to do well. Just before her daughter went to join the other athletes gathering at the start, Anne said a few final words of encouragement, reminding Megan about her technique and style.

But Megan was more than ready. She was desperate to run again. Today, she felt as though she could sprint all day and not grow tired. It was the best of feelings when it was like this. Megan thought of the great Usain Bolt and the way he looked when he ran. As she got down to her marks, she was smiling.

At the gun, Megan's confidence meant that there was no problem at all with her start and she was smoothly up from the blocks and quickly into her stride, running perfectly towards the first hurdle. She cleared it effortlessly and continued all the way up the straight in the same rhythmic style, brushing the top of two of the hurdles, but sailing over the rest.

Just as she had in the 100 metres, Megan led all the way and was not even put off her stride when the girl in the lane to her left crashed into a hurdle and went sprawling onto the track.

As Megan crossed the finish line, Anne punched the air, and shouted, 'Yes!'

Carole checked her stopwatch again and then raised her eyebrows as she saw the time. 'Wow!' she breathed.

Megan had done it – three out of three. When she came over to join Anne and Carole, she was almost bursting with joy.

Anne was even more excited. 'I told you.' she said. 'I've been telling everyone for ages. She's the next Denise Lewis or Jessica Ennis.'

Carole smiled. 'I don't know about that, but I do know that she's achieved the qualifying time for the UK championships, in two events. And I very much want her to be there.'

# Fourteen

Katy's house was not like Megan's.

Megan lived on a fairly new estate where all the homes were a little different and had front gardens with parking spaces or garages.

Katy's house was old, one of a long terrace of houses on a street where every home was almost identical. The houses were tall and thin, had front doors opening onto the pavement and long, narrow back gardens. Some had been converted into flats, but not Katy's.

Katy shared her home with her mum, Judy, her younger brothers, Alex and Billy, and a very friendly and boisterous dog called Ziggy, who constantly wagged his tail and seemed to be everyone's favourite member of the family.

The house was a little run-down and fairly untidy. It was noisy and busy and someone – usually followed by Ziggy – always seemed to be running up or down the steep wooden staircase searching for something that someone else had managed to lose.

It was all so warm and friendly that Megan loved being there from the moment she arrived. Everyone, even Ziggy, made her feel like one of the family.

Megan was visiting for a long weekend – the last weekend before school started again – and she was enjoying every moment.

Judy talked endlessly and was very funny, making Megan laugh all the time. She was very proud of all her children, and especially proud of Katy's achievements as an athlete. 'She doesn't take after me as a runner,' Judy said to Megan as they stood together in the kitchen. 'Must be her dad. He was a good runner.'

'Was he?' Megan said. 'Katy's never told me that.'

'Oh, yeah,' Judy said. 'He was terrific. He ran away from me quickly enough, didn't he?'

Megan stared for a moment, slightly shocked, and then saw that Judy was smiling. They both laughed.

'He could have broken the world record for running away,' Judy said, chuckling.

Judy had arranged a little party for that evening. It was no one's birthday and there was no special reason for celebrating. Judy had just decided that it was a great idea to have a party for her family and close friends, adults and children.

Everyone was helping with the preparations. Judy and Megan were making food in the kitchen, Katy had gone to the shops to buy the things that Judy had forgotten, the boys were tidying the house and garden – or were meant to be – and Ziggy was racing around, getting in the way.

The vacuum cleaner, which had been humming loudly for the past few minutes, suddenly fell silent, and then Alex wandered into the kitchen. 'I've done it,' he said to Judy. 'Looks great.'

Judy didn't look convinced. 'Shall we check, Megan?'

Megan smiled and nodded and followed them both through to the living room.

It didn't look sparkling clean or even particularly neat and tidy, but Judy just shrugged her shoulders. 'Not bad,' she said to Alex. She turned to Megan. 'Believe it or not, its a lot better than usual!'

A *little* party.

Megan laughed as she remembered what Judy had said. The house was packed!

The ground floor was rammed. People spilled from the living room through the hallway into the kitchen and out through the little conservatory into the back garden.

Judy and her children seemed to have so many relatives, all as friendly and smiley as they were. There were grandparents, aunts, uncles, cousins and second cousins. There were the people who weren't really related at all, but were called 'Uncle Terry' or 'Auntie Jane' or any number of other names that Megan was struggling to remember. Then there were the friends, so many of them, young and old.

Everyone seemed to be talking at the same time. Music blared from a set of speakers in the living room, while more speakers in the kitchen boomed the sounds out into the night through wide-open windows. No one was worried about upsetting any of the neighbours with loud music because all of the neighbours were at the party, having a great time.

Megan was having a great time, too. Katy had introduced her to all the cousins and friends and then, just to make sure she didn't feel left out, Alex and Billy had done the same thing. Ziggy was running around, tripping people up and then disappearing into the crowd before they had the chance to tell him off.

It was a baking hot, sticky, end-of-summer night; Megan had heard several people say there was a storm on the way. She'd lost sight of Katy for a while and decided to find her. Hot and thirsty, she squeezed her way through the crush in the living room into the hallway, then into the kitchen and finally the conservatory. But there was still no sign of Katy, so Megan went out into the garden.

It was dark outside, especially after the brightness inside the house. The air was thick and heavy, with not even a hint of a cooling breeze. Megan peered into the darkness and could just make out figures sitting on a bench near the end of the garden. She wondered if one of them might be Katy.

Megan moved closer and eventually heard low chatter and giggling. And then she saw that Katy wasn't there at all. One of her many cousins – a boy called Luke who Megan had met earlier – was talking to another boy she didn't recognise.

'Hiya,' Luke said, as Megan appeared out of the gloom. 'You all right?'

'I was looking for Katy,' Megan answered.

'She'll probably be out in a minute.' Luke nodded towards the other boy. 'This is my mate, Finn; he's just arrived.' He glanced at the gate at the end of the garden. 'He came in that way.'

'All right?' Finn said.

'I was looking for Katy,' Megan said again and then immediately felt silly as Finn laughed.

'You said that already.'

Megan was glad that the boys couldn't see her blushing in the darkness. They were older than her – about sixteen she guessed – and she felt awkward speaking to them. She was nervous and her mouth was dry. 'I think I'll go in and get a drink,' she said. 'I'm really thirsty.'

There was a sudden clanking of metal on metal as Finn raised up a clutch of tins held together by thin hoops of plastic. 'You don't need to go,' he said. 'I've got plenty here.'

Luke laughed. 'He brought them especially. Come and sit down.'

Megan hesitated. 'I ... I'd better...'

'It's all right, we don't bite.' Luke shuffled along the bench, leaving plenty of room at one end for Megan.

She stood rooted to the spot, feeling embarrassed. This was silly. Why shouldn't she sit on the bench with the two boys?

Megan stepped forward and perched herself on the edge of the bench. There was a short hissing sound as Finn pulled back the ringpull on one of the cans. He passed it to Megan.

'What is it?' Megan asked.

'Cider,' Finn said.

'Our favourite.' Luke laughed.

Megan went to give the can back. 'I don't drink cider.'

'Go on, it won't harm you,' Finn said. 'It's great when you're really thirsty, especially on a hot night like this.'

The tin felt cold in Megan's hands. 'I … I don't think so. I've never had alcohol.'

'There's hardly any alcohol in it,' Finn said. 'Go on, give it a try. We won't tell anyone.'

Megan was very thirsty and her mouth was becoming drier by the second. Tentatively, she put her lips to the can. She took a sip and felt the cool liquid trickle down her parched throat.

# Fifteen

The whole world was spinning and Megan was spinning with it. It was as though her entire body was turning through a complete circle, moving slowly up and over and around and down. And when she reached the bottom and completed the circle she was sick again.

She hung her head over the toilet bowl and groaned as the tears streamed down her face and into her mouth. It was so awful, terrible, horrible. She couldn't remember ever feeling so bad.

'It's all right, Megan, love,' Judy said, stroking her hair. 'We'll get you into bed in a minute. You'll feel better then.'

At that moment, Megan believed that she would never ever feel better and her world started to spin yet again.

Katy was kneeling on the floor close to Megan. She was in tears, too. 'I'm so sorry, Meg. So, sorry.'

'It's not your fault,' Megan just managed to say before throwing up again.

'No, it's not Katy's fault,' Judy said angrily before turning back and glaring at a figure standing in the doorway. 'It's yours!'

Luke swallowed nervously. 'I'm sorry, Aunt Jude,' he said sheepishly. 'I didn't think she had that much. And I did come and find you when she said that she felt ill. And…'

'You should never have given it to her. And you shouldn't be drinking yourself at your age.'

'It was only…'

'I don't care what it was,' Judy snapped. 'You knew that I wouldn't allow alcohol so you got your friend to sneak in at the back gate with it. And then you hid at the bottom of the garden so that no one would see you.'

'We didn't hide, not really. And I've said I'm sorry, Aunt Jude.'

A clap of thunder overhead seemed to rock the house. The summer heat had finally broken and rain was pouring down, beating against the bathroom window. A streak of lightning flashed across the sky and lit up Judy's eyes as she glared at her young nephew.

'Go away, Luke. I don't want to see you right now. And I wouldn't want to be in your shoes when your mum catches up with you.'

Luke sighed and walked slowly away just as Megan groaned loudly.

'There, there, love,' Judy said, stroking her hair. 'You'll feel better soon, really.'

Another clap of thunder rumbled and rolled around the sky and Megan felt as though it was inside her pounding head.

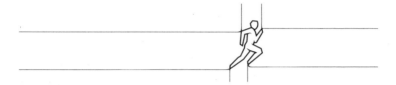

Megan was eating a slice of dry toast. She didn't really want it, but Judy had insisted she eat something. Dry toast was all she could face. Her head was still thumping and she was even thirstier than before she'd drunk the cider on the previous evening.

Cider. Megan shuddered. She knew she would never ever drink cider again. Even the thought of it made her feel ill. The taste and the smell still seemed to linger in her mouth and her nostrils. She shivered. All she wanted to drink now was water, litres and litres of cold, clear water. She picked up her glass and drank quickly, but when the glass was empty she still felt thirsty.

Outside, the sun was shining on a clear, bright morning. The night's storm had driven away the heavy atmosphere, but the mood in the kitchen was gloomy.

Katy sat opposite her friend, looking worried. She picked up a bottle of mineral water, refilled Megan's empty glass and then glanced over at her mum who was standing by the door.

'I do have to tell your parents what happened,' Judy said to Megan. She smiled sympathetically as the pale-faced young girl lifted her head and looked at her with red-rimmed eyes. 'You're staying with me, so I'm responsible for you. You do understand that, don't you, love?'

Megan went to speak but her mouth was so dry no words would come out. So she just nodded.

Judy went over to Megan and gave her a comforting squeeze on one shoulder. 'I'll call them now,' she said and went quickly into the living room.

Megan felt so silly. Everyone was being as considerate and sensitive as possible. But somehow, the kindness and consideration only made her feel worse.

Alex and Billy had both been in to ask how she was feeling before uttering a few sympathetic words and then slipping quietly away. Ziggy the dog lay under the table, for once on his very best behaviour. Even his tail was still. It was almost as if he knew Megan was unwell.

'I was stupid,' she said, remembering how she had gulped down the cider. 'And I didn't even like the taste.' Chewing on the toast and swallowing it was so difficult. She really couldn't finish a whole slice. She put the last piece back onto her plate. 'I made such a fool of myself.'

'No, you didn't,' Katy said softly. 'It was just one of those things. It happens to everyone.'

'Has it happened to you?' asked Megan.

'Well … well, no, but…'

'That's because you're not stupid like me, Katy.'

Katy sipped at her tea and then banged down the cup harder than she meant to. Megan flinched and closed her eyes tightly at the sound.

'I'm so sorry, Meg,' Katy said quickly. 'I didn't mean to … your headache…'

'It's all right,' Megan said, opening her eyes. 'I deserve it.'

'No, you don't!' Katy snapped. She lowered her voice. 'I'm so cross with Luke and that friend of his. Finn wasn't even invited to the party.'

Some of Katy's tea had spilled onto the kitchen table. She went to the sink, grabbed a cloth and wiped the liquid from the tabletop.

'It wasn't really their fault,' Megan said. 'I could have said that I didn't want the drink. I don't know why I didn't. I was embarrassed, I suppose. And they were just having a laugh.'

'At your expense,' Katy said. 'I'll never speak to Luke again. Never.'

Megan took another long drink of water. She put the glass gently back down on the table, wondering what was being said in the phone conversation between

Judy and her parents.

She didn't have to wait long to find out.

Soon after, the door to the hallway opened and Judy walked in. She raised her eyebrows as the girls looked at her and then sat at the table. 'Pour me a cup of tea, love,' she said to Katy. 'I need one.'

Megan's head was still thumping. 'Who did you speak to?' she said to Judy.

'I'm afraid that your mum answered the phone,' Judy replied with a sad shake of her head. 'I didn't have any choice.'

'Oh, no,' Megan groaned.

Katy placed a cup of tea in front of her mum and both girls watched as Judy slowly stirred in a spoonful of sugar, looking very thoughtful. She sipped at her drink and sighed. 'She didn't take it well, love,' she said to Megan. She swallowed another much-needed mouthful of tea and then sighed for a second time. 'Not at all well.'

Megan put her head in her hands and stared down at the table. Her headache was suddenly even more painful.

# Sixteen

Megan was meant to stay at Katy's until late afternoon, but as soon as Anne heard the news about the party she told Judy that she was coming to collect her daughter immediately.

When Anne arrived she said very little but acted swiftly. She refused Judy's offer of a cup of tea, grabbed Megan's rucksack, told her daughter to thank Judy and Katy for the visit and then stomped off and got back in the car.

Megan gave Katy and Judy a hug, smiled at the boys, patted Ziggy on the head and then walked to the car and got in. As Anne sped away, Megan gazed from her window and saw Katy and her family waving sadly. She waved back, equally sadly. The smiles and laughter of the previous day had disappeared.

Anne looked furious for the entire journey and most of the time acted as if Megan wasn't there. Megan tried to speak once but all Anne would say was, 'Later, Megan. I'm too angry to speak to you now.'

The journey seemed to last for hours because of the

endless silence; Anne wouldn't even let Megan switch on the radio.

It was around lunchtime when they arrived home. Megan went into the house through the kitchen door as she usually did.

Her dad was there. He was cooking and he smiled when he saw Megan. 'How are you?'

'Not great,' Megan replied with a shrug of her shoulders.

'I'm cooking a proper Sunday lunch. Roast beef, roast potatoes, the lot. Want some?'

Megan's stomach churned. The thought of food – any food – was still enough to make her want to heave. 'I don't think so, Dad.'

John gave his daughter a sympathetic smile. He winked at her. 'How about a glass of cider, then?'

Anne walked in just before he said it and her eyes widened in horror as the words emerged. 'Oh, that's right,' she snarled. 'Make a joke of it, just like you always do. Everything's just one big joke, isn't it? Even when it's something as serious as this.'

'I'm sorry,' John said quickly. 'I didn't mean start an argument. I was just trying…'

'No, you never do. That's the trouble.'

'Look, it's not that bad, Anne. All right, Megan did something stupid and I'm sure she regrets it, but…'

'Not that bad! I can't believe you can take this so

lightly. She got drunk, that's bad enough. And on top of that, she's probably ruined all the hard work we've put into her training over the past few months.'

'Oh, that's ridiculous! And you're overreacting as usual, Anne! It was a crazy thing to do and she'll be grounded for a while. But that's enough.'

Megan's head was swimming and her stomach continued to churn. The last thing she needed now was another argument between her parents, especially one that involved her athletics. She slumped down onto a kitchen chair and put her head in her hands.

'Look at her!' Anne snapped. 'What a mess. I should never have let her go.' She glared at Megan. 'That's the last time you go there, I can promise you. You're finished with Katy after this.'

At that moment, Megan felt too weary and unwell to argue, so she didn't even reply.

But her mum still had plenty to say, particularly to John. 'How can she train and prepare for the most important races in her life when she's in this state?'

John's anger was also spilling out. 'Athletics! Races! It always comes back to that, doesn't it? That's all that matters to you.'

Both parents were shouting now and as Megan listened, tears began to roll down her face.

'It should be important to her!' Anne yelled. 'And at least I care about something, which is more than you ever do about anything.'

'Oh, I care, all right!' John yelled back. 'But I care in the right way. Not like you. You're obsessed, totally obsessed. This isn't about Megan. It's about *you*!'

Suddenly, Megan stood up, sending the kitchen chair clattering loudly across the tiled floor. 'Shut up!' she shouted. 'Just shut up, will you? Both of you!'

Both parents stared in stunned silence. Megan had never spoken like this to either of them. She didn't want to now, but something inside had snapped. 'All you ever do is argue! Argue, argue, argue!'

Anne went to speak, quietly this time. 'Megan...'

'And I've had enough!' Megan yelled. And before either parent could say another word she ran from the kitchen, slammed the door behind her and raced up the stairs to her room.

Anne glared at John as they heard Megan's bedroom door slam shut. 'Now look what you've done!' she snarled. 'I suppose you're happy now!'

# Seventeen

Megan missed training for two days; she just didn't feel like doing it and her mum didn't even mention it. The atmosphere at home was as cold as ice, with Anne and John ignoring each other and Megan mainly staying in her room and preparing for her return to school.

When the family did meet, at mealtimes or in the evenings in front of the television, there was an awkward and uncomfortable silence, and Megan was relieved when the first day of term arrived.

She had often swapped texts with Ellie and Beth during the long holiday, but so much had been happening that she hadn't actually seen either of her friends since before their Spanish adventure. So when they met at school, there was so much to talk about, and Ellie was especially keen to tell Megan all about their time in sunny Spain. The holiday seemed to have made the two girls even closer friends and Megan couldn't help feeling a little jealous as they spoke about the wonderful time they'd enjoyed.

Everything had been just brilliant and the girls were already talking about returning to Spain the following summer. But this time there was no mention of Megan joining them. It was as though they had already accepted that her running would come first and there was no point asking her.

Megan felt even more left out and was pleased when lessons began and there was something else for them all to concentrate on. But she felt strangely lonely all day, even though she was with her friends for most of the time.

When she got home from school, Anne asked her, without much enthusiasm, if she wanted to train that evening. Megan simply nodded and trudged miserably up to her room to change.

Her dad was in the kitchen when she came back down, and as Megan glanced through the kitchen window she saw that her mum was already waiting in the car.

'Your mum, eh?' John said to Megan. 'What is she like? I think it's all getting a bit out of hand, don't you?'

'Dad!' Megan snapped. 'It's not just Mum, and don't expect me to take sides in this.'

She stomped off and went out to the car. By the time they arrived at the track, many athletes were already training.

The chief coach, Danny, was working with a group of young sprinters. 'All right, Meg?' he called as Megan and Anne jogged by at the start of their warm-up.

Megan nodded and smiled, but she didn't feel all right.

'Can't wait to see you run in the championships!' Danny shouted as they continued around the track. 'We'll all be cheering for you.'

The young sprinters with Danny all decided to give Megan a loud cheer to speed her on her way. She turned and waved back at them, trying to look more cheerful that she felt.

'All those youngsters are supporting you and you let them down,' Anne said quietly without even looking at Megan. 'I don't think they'd be cheering so loudly if they knew what you did last weekend.'

Megan stopped jogging and stared at her mum, who had also come to a standstill.

'Mum,' Megan said, 'are we ever going to get over this? Didn't you ever make a mistake? Ever?'

'This isn't about me, Megan,' Anne answered.

'Isn't it?' Megan realised right then that she was totally fed up of feeling bad. 'Maybe Dad's right. Maybe this has been all about you since I first started running.' And before her mum had a chance to reply, she sprinted away towards the changing room.

'Megan!' Anne called after her. 'Megan, wait!'

Anne looked back and saw that Danny and the young sprinters were staring at her. She felt herself blushing so she turned away and walked quickly off the track.

The week didn't get better.

At home, no one – not Anne nor John, nor even Megan – said, 'Let's sit down and talk about it.'

All three had hurt feelings. And all three were thinking that it was up to the other two to make them feel better. And the longer the situation went on, the more difficult it became.

Megan didn't really want to go into her problems with Ellie and Beth. She'd spoken to them often about the different ways her mum and dad felt about her athletics. And she had a feeling that if she mentioned it again, they would simply say, 'We've heard it all before, Meg. Just get it sorted.' But she couldn't get it sorted.

At school she pretended that everything was fine, laughing and joking with her friends, talking about the things they always talked about and getting on with her schoolwork. But inside she was feeling more and more miserable.

There was only one highlight in the whole grim

week. It happened on the Friday, when she took the programme from the Liverpool v Barcelona match to school, so that she could show it to Gavin Richards.

She found him at lunchtime, and when she took the programme from her bag and handed it over, Gavin's jaw dropped and his eyes widened.

'You ... you were there?' he gasped.

Megan nodded and smiled. 'It was a great match; I really enjoyed it. Finished two all.'

'I know,' Gavin said, carefully turning the pages of the programme as though it were the most valuable document in the world.

'You can have it if you want.'

Gavin looked up, his eyes even wider. 'You're ... you're joking, right?'

'No,' Megan said. 'I've read it and I thought you might like it.'

Gavin seemed lost for words. He looked at the programme and then at Megan and then back at the programme. Finally, he managed to speak. 'Megan ... you are ... that is ... I mean ... it's ... like ... thanks, Megan. You are awesome.'

Awesome.

Megan laughed. She didn't feel awesome. She still felt unhappy. And confused. And lonely. But she decided at that moment that she was going to do something about it.

# Eighteen

John's hands were trembling as he read the hastily written letter for the third time.

> Dear Mum and Dad,
>
> I'm sorry everything has been so horrible and I'm sorry you are both so upset. I've decided I'm giving up athletics for ever because it makes us all so unhappy. Don't worry about me. I'll be fine.
>
> Love,
> Megan
> xxx

The door to the hallway opened and Anne came in looking pale-faced and worried. 'Some of her clothes have gone; she must have packed them into her training bag. And the money she's been saving has gone, too.'

'How much money?'

'I don't know. She's been saving for quite a while. John, we don't even know what time she left.'

Her husband glanced up at the clock. It was six in the evening. 'She can't have gone far. We'll call her friends. You try Ellie and I'll call Beth.'

'We should call the police.'

'There's no point yet. They won't be able to do anything until she's been missing for hours.'

Anne's eyes filled with tears. 'Oh, John…'

'Let's not panic. There's no need, not yet.'

'It's our fault. We've driven her to this.'

John wrapped his arms around Anne. 'And there's no point in blaming ourselves, either. Let's find her and bring her home, then we'll sort it out. You have tried her mobile?'

Anne nodded. 'It just goes straight to voicemail. She must have switched it off.'

'Did you leave a message?'

'Yes. Nothing angry, just asking her to call us. And to come home.'

'I'll try it again. Then we'll call her friends.' But when John called Megan's mobile phone, it went straight through to voicemail again.

They called Ellie and Beth, trying to sound as calm

as possible, asking if Megan was with them as she hadn't arrived home.

Both girls said they hadn't seen Megan since leaving school, but that they would call back if Megan contacted them.

'What about her friend, Katy?' John said to Anne.

'In Liverpool? Surely she wouldn't go all that way on her own?' said Anne.

'But maybe she's phoned Katy, or sent her a text. I'll try her home number.'

Judy answered the phone and was horrified to hear that Megan was missing. She asked Katy if she knew anything. Katy said that she'd had texts from Megan during the week, but no calls. Neither of them had any idea where Megan was.

As Anne listened to John speaking on the telephone she knew that she should be talking to Judy. So as John was about to end the call, she took the telephone from him. 'Judy,' she said quickly, 'I'm so, so sorry about last weekend. It was stupid of me, and now it's caused all this.'

'Last weekend doesn't matter one bit,' Judy answered kindly. 'All that matters now is that we find Megan.'

They spoke for a few minutes and Judy promised to call if they heard anything at all. 'And you will let us know if there's any news, won't you?' she asked.

'Of course we will,' Anne said. 'I promise.'

John was putting on a jacket. 'I'm going out in the car to look for her,' he said to Anne. 'You stay here by the phone. Call me if Megan rings.' He put his arms around Anne and they hugged each other tightly. 'She's all right, Anne. I know she is. And we'll find her.'

It had been a long, tiring journey. Megan wasn't even certain which station to ask for when she bought her train ticket at Wrexham. She eventually decided on Liverpool Lime Street, because the man in the ticket office said it was the main city station in Liverpool.

She waited for the train, thinking perhaps that at any moment her mum and dad would come running onto the platform to beg her to come home.

But they didn't.

When the train pulled in, Megan was glad to get on. She found a seat and stared sadly from the window as the countryside whizzed past. At Bidston, she had to change to another train and she eventually arrived at Liverpool Lime Street at around eight-thirty.

The station was still busy and as Megan wearily battled her way through the crowds she realised that although she knew Katy's address, she had no idea how to get there.

The only answer was a taxi. Megan followed the signs and when she got outside made her way to the front of a long line of black cabs. The taxi driver gave her a smile as she peered through the window at him. 'Hello, love,' he said. 'You okay?'

Megan nodded. She read out Katy's address from the piece of paper she'd written it on and asked the driver if he could take her there.

'I can, love,' he said. 'But that's quite a way. Are you sure you've got enough money to pay for it?'

'How much will it be, please?'

The driver shrugged his shoulders. 'Maybe seventeen or eighteen pounds.'

'That's okay,' Megan said, breathing a sigh of relief. 'I've got enough.'

The driver smiled. 'Jump in, then.'

Megan got into the taxi and settled onto the comfortable seat. She had twenty-five pounds left of her savings. It would almost all be gone by the time she arrived at Katy's, but she didn't care. She just wanted to be there.

The journey through the busy city streets seemed to take forever as the taxi edged its way through long queues of traffic. Once or twice, Megan noticed the driver looking at her in the rear-view mirror. He seemed worried. 'Are you sure you're okay?' he asked after a while.

'Yes, thank you,' she answered.

'Where you going, then?'

'To visit my friend.'

'Oh, right. That's nice. And your mum and dad, they know you're visiting this friend, do they?'

Megan crossed her fingers on both hands. She hated telling lies of any sort, but she didn't really have a choice. 'Oh, yes,' she said.

When the taxi finally pulled up outside Katy's house, the metre read £18.60, but the driver refused to take any more than fifteen pounds from Megan. He watched as she walked over to Katy's front door and waited until it opened before driving away.

Katy and Judy were both standing there in the doorway. 'Megan!' they yelled together.

From somewhere inside the house, Megan heard Ziggy bark excitedly. And for the first time in a long while, she smiled.

Anne put down the phone. She was shaking and crying, but her tears were of joy and relief.

'She's fine,' she said to John. 'Just tired. And Judy said she was really hungry when she arrived. She's going to bed soon. I thought it was best that I didn't insist on speaking to her now.'

John smiled with relief. 'You did the right thing. And I'm glad you agreed to Megan staying there until tomorrow.'

'I've been getting so much wrong, John,' Anne replied wearily. She sat on the sofa next to him and he put an arm around her.

For a while neither of them said a thing. And then John leaned over and kissed Anne gently on the cheek. 'We've both been getting it wrong,' he said softly.

# Nineteen

Sometimes on a Saturday morning, Megan loved to stay in her pyjamas long after getting up. It was so comforting, especially if she'd been unwell or had been feeling down. Fortunately for Megan, Katy felt exactly the same way.

After she arrived, Megan had spoken to Katy and her mum for a long time, spilling out her worries and fears and telling them that she'd decided she was giving up athletics. It was the only way that her family could be happy again, she told them.

Judy and Katy said nothing to try to make Megan change her mind and eventually the two girls trooped wearily up the stairs to bed. They'd both fallen asleep very quickly.

They slept late into the morning. Then they crept downstairs to find that Judy was up and about and that the boys were out taking Ziggy for a walk. The previous day had been exhausting so when Katy asked her mum if they could take some toast and big glasses of orange juice back up to bed, Judy was happy to agree.

'Don't spill the orange juice,' she said, pretending to be threatening. 'Or else!'

The girls laughed.

'I've got lots to do anyway,' Judy added a little mysteriously.

The girls took up their toast and juice on trays, and while they relaxed and chatted in Katy's bedroom, Judy got busy. First she called Megan's parents and told them about the plan she had been forming. They were happy to go along with the idea so then she made a second call.

When the girls finally came down, dressed at last, Judy had made lunch. The boys and Ziggy were back, and while everyone got stuck into the meal, the dog lay patiently under the table.

No one mentioned what had happened, but when lunch was almost over Judy said to Megan, 'I told your parents that I'd take you back this evening. Is that okay, love?'

Megan nodded. 'Are they angry with me?' she asked a little anxiously.

'Of course not.' Judy smiled. 'They're just looking forward to seeing you.'

While Megan and the boys washed up and put away the plates and dishes, Judy grabbed a quiet word with Katy.

By the time Megan had put the last of the dishes into the correct cupboard, Katy was in the living room, curled up on the sofa in front of the television. Megan went through to join her and Ziggy followed. He flopped down on the carpet and gazed up at the girls, as if to say, 'Now what are we going to do?'

Katy knew exactly what they were going to do. A sports programme was on television, but Katy had the remote control in one hand. She switched over to the DVD player and then pressed the play button. 'Mum bought me this last Christmas,' she said innocently, without even looking at Megan.

It was a film of athletes in action, some of the greatest-ever sprinters winning Olympic gold. For a moment, Megan thought about asking Katy to turn it off. After all, she was giving up athletics, which meant she didn't really want to watch this. But she was in Katy's house; it would be rude to tell her friend what to do.

They watched in silence for a while and Megan tried not to be swept up in the excitement. There were brilliant runs going back through Olympic Games of the past twenty years or more, and as she watched, Megan couldn't stop her old enthusiasm from flooding back.

Katy said nothing. She just watched and smiled to herself as she saw how the film was thrilling her friend. Finally they reached the gold-medal-winning runs of Megan's great hero, Usain Bolt.

Megan had seen the 100 metres where he shattered the world record dozens of times, but as the runners got down into their blocks she was on the edge of her seat and almost bursting with anticipation, as excited as if she had never seen it before.

She cheered the Lightning Bolt all the way down the straight and jumped for joy when he crossed the finish line and raised both arms in triumph.

When she turned to look at Katy, her friend was smiling at her. 'You don't really want to give up athletics, do you, Meg?'

They were all sitting at the kitchen table: Megan, her mum and dad, Judy and Katy, and Carole.

Carole was the other person Judy had called that morning. At first, the coach had been unsure about Judy's plan, saying that if Megan really did want to give up athletics then she should be allowed to do exactly that. No one should force her to continue with the sport.

But that was before Katy and Megan had watched the DVD. And that was before Megan had said for certain that she did want to carry on running and that her dream to one day be an Olympic athlete was as strong as ever.

Judy quickly called Carole back and then it was Carole's turn to get busy on the telephone. Now, she just had to explain the plan to Megan.

'So,' Carole said, 'I've had a long chat with your parents and a long chat with Danny, the head coach at your club.'

'Danny?' said Megan, looking confused. 'Why Danny?'

Carole glanced at Anne, who smiled and nodded for her to continue.

'We've all agreed that it would be a good idea for Danny to look after your sprint training for a while. And while he's doing that, your mum is going to be coaching some of the other young athletes at the club.'

Megan stared at her mum. 'Really? Is that true?'

Anne laughed. 'I think it's a great idea. We all do.'

'And that does mean all of us,' Megan's dad added. 'We all want you to do as well as you possibly can at the championships.'

'You're going to have to work hard with Danny,' Carole said. 'You've lost training time and the championships are coming up very soon.'

Anne took one of Megan's hands and squeezed it gently. 'If you still want to compete that is.'

Megan smiled. 'I do, Mum,' she said. 'I really do.'

# Twenty

Everyone was waiting for the final. Carole had come from Manchester, Judy and Katy had travelled from Liverpool, Danny was prowling around with other anxious coaches, even Ellie and Beth had squeezed into the car with Megan and her parents so that they could be there, too. This was it, the biggest race of Megan's young life.

The stadium was packed, crammed full, and nerves were jangling as the start of the race came closer and closer. But Megan was completely calm. She felt great, confident, ready to fly.

And as the minutes ticked down, the more certain Megan became that this was what she wanted; out here on the track was where she belonged. All the doubts and conflicts of the previous weeks had disappeared. Megan now knew that she was a true athlete; her sport was natural to her, it was part of her.

The London 2012 Olympic Games moved ever nearer, and with every passing day Megan became more determined to realise her own Olympic dream. The next Games were in Rio de Janeiro in Brazil in 2016, and Megan had made up her mind – she was going to be there.

She took a deep breath and peered up into the main grandstand to where her family and friends were sitting. She saw them wave and she smiled and waved back, and at that moment the thoughts of all that had happened over the past few weeks flashed through her mind.

So much had changed. A new coach, a new attitude from both her parents – everything was so much better now.

And most importantly for Megan, everyone was supporting her in the right way, not pushing but encouraging, exactly what she needed.

Danny had sensibly decided that because of the lost time they would focus on just one event, the 100 metres. And it was a good decision, because Megan had swept through to the final.

And now the final was just moments away. Megan was at the starting area with the other runners. Some were pacing anxiously like caged lions, some stood rooted to the spot but twitched their legs or an arm as they gazed down the track. Others stared wide-eyed, whispering to themselves, seeing in their minds every stride of the race.

Megan stood completely still, breathing steadily and deeply. She looked down at her starting blocks. She had practised her start several times and each time had been perfect. She was ready. She was totally focused. There was nothing more she could do but run.

'On your marks!'

Megan was in lane five. She walked forward, stared down the lane to the finish and then got into her start position. Her feet settled into her blocks and her fingers were placed firmly behind the line. She rocked from side to side a couple of times and then was still. Other runners took longer to settle. The girl on Megan's left took the longest of all, fidgeting and twitching for long seconds before finally being still. Megan tried to ignore everything around her, thinking only of her own start and her own race.

The packed stadium was absolutely silent. Up in the stand, Anne made herself breathe slowly to help fight back her own nerves. John stared anxiously at the track and crossed his fingers. Beth and Ellie held hands and Judy gave Katy an encouraging smile.

'Set!'

Megan raised herself up, poised to spring forward, but noticing again that the girl on her left was the last to rise and be still. Some runners used this tactic to deliberately unsettle their rivals. That thought flashed into Megan's mind but she forced it away, telling herself that this was no time to think about anything but...

Crack!

It came so suddenly, the starting pistol; Megan had allowed another thought to break her concentration. She leapt into her race, but instantly knew that she was slower out of her blocks than all of the other girls. It was a terrible start and no one's fault but her own.

Megan's family and friends were on their feet, like everyone else around them in the grandstand.

'Oh, no!' John groaned.

Ellie and Beth squeezed each other's hands; even they could see that Megan was the last girl into her running and in last place after the first ten metres.

Anne clenched both hands tightly, willing her daughter on. 'Don't panic, Meg,' she whispered. 'Just run. Run!'

Megan wasn't panicking. She wasn't even angry with herself. There was no time and no room in Megan's mind for panic. She knew a race was never lost until it was over.

At the twenty-metre mark her long elegant stride was perfect, her legs lifting high and her arms pumping backward and forward.

'Go, Meg, go!' Katy shouted as her friend battled up the straight.

'Run, love!' yelled Judy, grasping her daughter's hand. 'You can do it!'

And Megan was clawing her way back into the race. Her running action was beautiful as she swept past two of the girls.

But a 100-metres race is over in seconds, and Megan was still behind the leaders at the forty-metre mark.

Then, to the watching crowd, it was almost as though Megan had found another gear as she accelerated, moving faster than every other girl in the race.

A smile spread across Carole's face. 'Beautiful,' she breathed. 'Beautiful.'

Anne's eyes were misting with tears. 'That's my girl,' she whispered.

There were thirty metres to go. Megan felt wonderful. Amazing. Incredible.

Twenty metres now.

'You can do it, Meg!' yelled John.

Ten metres. She was up with the leaders; she was flying.

'Go, go, go!' screamed Katy. 'Go!'

Five metres, then three, then one, then…

Megan dipped forward as she crossed the finishing line and she knew. She'd done it.

This was it, the very best feeling. She was smiling, beaming and then laughing out loud as she raised both arms in triumph.